JUN

2010

THE MAN FROM CODY COUNTY

Lauran Paine who, under his own name and various pseudonyms has written over 900 books, was born in Duluth, Minnesota. His family moved to California when he was at an early age and his apprenticeship as a Western writer came about through the years he spent in the livestock trade, rodeos, and even motion pictures—where he served as an extra because of his expert horsemanship in several films starring movie cowboy Johnny Mack Brown. In the late 1930s, Paine trapped wild horses in northern Arizona and, for a time, worked as a professional farrier. Paine came to know the old West through the eyes of many who had been born in the previous century and he learned that Western life had been very different from the way it was portrayed on the screen. "I knew men who had killed other men," he later recalled. "But they were the exceptions. Prior to and during the Depression, people were just too busy eking out an existence to indulge in Saturday-night brawls." He served in the U.S. Navy in the Second World War and began writing for Western pulp magazines following his discharge. It is interesting to note that all of his earliest novels (written under his own name and the pseudonym Mark Carrel) were published in the British market and he soon had as strong a following in that country as in the United States. Paine's Western fiction is characterized by strong plots, authenticity, an apparently effortless ability to construct situation and character, and a preference for building his stories upon a solid foundation of historical fact. *Adobe Empire* (1956), one of his best novels, is a fictionalized account of the last twenty years in the life of trader William Bent and, in an off-trail way, has a melancholy, bittersweet texture that is not easily forgotten. In later novels like *The White Bird* (1997) and *Cache Cañon* (1998), he showed that the special magic and power of his stories and characters had only matured along with his basic themes of changing times, changing attitudes, learning from experience, respecting Nature, and the yearning for a simpler, more moderate way of life. The film *Open Range* (Buena Vista, 2003), based on Paine's 1990 novel, starring Robert Duvall, Kevin Costner, and Annette Bening became an international success.

THE MAN FROM CODY COUNTY

Lauran Paine

GUNSMOKE

First published in the UK by Hale

This hardback edition 2010
by BBC Audiobooks Ltd
by arrangement with
Golden West Literary Agency

ISBN 978 1 408 46267 6

British Library Cataloguing in Publication Data available.

Printed and bound in Great Britain by
CPI Antony Rowe, Chippenham and Eastbourne

Chapter One

WHERE the trail forked there were two signs, each pointing in a different direction, each with a different name upon it. The town to the east was called White Mountain, the one to the west was called Grasshopper. The man from Wyoming grinned at the sign pointing westerly. He was already riding the White Mountains, so a town by the same name sounded neither imaginative nor interesting. But a place called Grasshopper held promise. He took the westward trail.

In Arizona there were two kinds of people and three kinds of land : Honest people and dishonest people; wet land, dry land, and sand. A man passing through Arizona once said the land was divided between hot and hotter; and of course, while he was correct enough in summertime, Arizona was far from being the desert of endless thirst and torment such a facetious designation implied. But folks being folks, they believed that Arizona was a big blank space in a bigger, blanker space called The West. Their prejudices persevered. Arizona didn't get into the U.S. Federal Union as a state until 1912. Not because it didn't have good farms, rivers, high mountains with pines and plenty of snow, but because the facetious remarks about it prejudiced people against Arizona who'd never been west of the Hudson or south of the Rapahannock. In a few words, while thousands of families migrated to Oregon and Northern California, a very, very slim trickle went down into Arizona, and that trickle was almost exclusively men like Anvil Wilson, the man from Cody County, Wyoming.

Anvil wasn't his real name. After custom his parents had given Anvil as his first name his mother's maiden name, which had been Arnwell. Through contraction, distortion, and just plain cussedness down the years, Arnwell became Anvil.

Anvil Wilson was a quiet-eyed lean man with a lilt of humour at the outer corners of his wide mouth. He was one of those men who could've been twenty or forty. But two things a person noticed about Anvil right off. One; he was durable. It stood out in the way he moved and acted and even in the way he smiled. Anvil Wilson had survived hardship, peril, hunger, freeze and heat, with that faint little quirked-up smile of his. He was wise in the many ways of survival. And two; Anvil Wilson was a killer. It was difficult to explain how an observer would know that, but in lawless Arizona folks had ways of sensing things.

Gunfighters weren't always dressed in black, with eyes like wolves and tempers like the spring of a lion trap. They came in as endless a variety of humankind as did miners or merchants or even cattlemen. Sometimes they smiled easily, just like anyone else; sometimes they even smiled when they pulled the trigger. But a smile by itself means nothing. It's what a man does while he's smiling that gives the smile its form and substance and significance, for unlike a scowl, a smile is the most treacherous of all human facial expressions. A scowl means only one thing: Disapproval. But a smile can hide treachery, duplicity, or plain murder.

Anvil's smile was always just below the surface. Even when he was riding a lonely trail, there lay a hint of it down around his mouth. It could have meant that Anvil's disposition was affable and friendly. That faint suggestion of good humour made it easy for folks to cotton to Anvil Wilson at first sight. Even that first camp he'd made in the White Mountains, which have traditionally been Apache country for generations and therefore none too hospitable towards outlanders, made him an acquaintance, because he smiled at the stocky Indian who sat his horse as still as stone back in the forest, until Anvil had spoken to him quietly and casually without even looking around, and when the buck had ridden up, Anvil had grinned.

From that White Mountain Apache he'd learned about the split in the trail. He also learned that at White Mountain there was an Indian Agency, a company of lazy soldiers, a deputy federal marshal to keep order instead of a local sheriff because White Mountain was a government preserve, and that over at Grasshopper there was none of these things.

Something else he learned from the buck was that, since the Mexican border wasn't far off, when the Indians got tired of cultivating their maize and squash plots, they'd sneak down there, raise a little hell, and sneak back again, and although the Mex authorities invariably exaggerated each little raid out of all proportion to fact, and lodged protests in Washington, D.C., by the time that U.S. deputy marshal got instructions to arrest the offenders over at White Mountain, no one could recall who they were.

Anvil and the buck laughed about that, drinking Anvil's coffee and eating his tinned beef at the campfire. Later, as Anvil was approaching Grasshopper, alone and at a leisurely gait, he saw that same buck Indian sitting on a pine-scented slope watching the trail. Anvil waved. The Indian waved back. Such was the soft magic of a gunfighter's smile.

Grasshopper wasn't much of a place. Once, so the

story went, Apachedom's great leaders Mangas Colorados and his kinsman Cochise, had preferred that spot for their permanent camps because of the elevation, the surrounding mountains, and the good water, which was always cold even in midsummer when the land writhed and shimmered.

Whether that was true or not didn't change the one basic fact of the legend: The water was cold, even in midsummer. Anvil tested it where the trail dipped down and passed across a humid, green glade. The creek there was wide enough for a horse to step across, but it was nearly three feet deep, full of clean pebbles and water cold enough to make a man draw back after only a few swallows.

Beyond, where Grasshopper lay, there were enfolding hills and farther back, dark-forested mountains. The town itself wasn't much, but then it had no reason to be; if there were big cow outfits in the Grasshopper country they didn't appear to trade at Grasshopper, and if there were mines, they too seemed hidden.

Anvil saw some cattle, mostly of the hooked-horned Mexican variety, slab-sided, ridge-backed, orry-eyed and nearly as long-legged as a saddlehorse. He thought they were probably descendants of animals oldtime marauding Apaches had come racing up out of Mexico with, until he saw some of those unmistakable, spidery Mexican brands. He grinned at that; evidently all the 'Pache raiders hadn't died out after old Naná and Geronimo had been crushed.

Grasshopper didn't have a liverybarn, it had a big public corral instead. It didn't have a hotel either, but there were any number of louse-infested old hogans scattered around which were more or less community property. That is, if a man didn't object to living in the conical, bee-hive, low-roofed brush shelters of Apacheria, which were dark as sin inside and ordinarily harboured at least one rattlesnake, dozens of large hairy spiders, and smelled to high heaven of their former occupants, a people to whom cleanliness was less of a virtue than it was the natural aftermath of having to wade across rivers now and then.

There was a general store in Grasshopper, the focal point of nearly all local life. There was also a black-smith shop, a log jailhouse, a café, a saloon, and several other business establishments, all very elemental in their purpose, all indicative of the existence of whiteskins in the area.

When Anvil rode in it was midday. Heat layered the outlying slopes like varying depths of transparent oil. When a vagrant, rare breeze crested the mountains and tumbled headlong down the trough of the hills, the waves sluggishly heaved and writhed. There were some small boys playing in the hot mud beside a public water trough that leaked at each seam. Mud-dauber wasps flitted around them menacingly but the children, as brown as old leather with the moon-faces and fathomless black eyes of Apaches, completely ignored the wasps to glance up as Anvil came along. Little boys are the same the world over; these stared. They drew back a little when Anvil got down and slipped the bridle to water his horse, and silently stared. They were very candid about it. Strangers riding into Grasshopper weren't exactly unheard of, but they weren't exactly commonplace either. There was no place to go after a man reached Grasshopper, except up into the brooding forests or back the way he'd come, and without dance halls or gambling rooms and only one dilapidated saloon, there wasn't much to hold a man in Grasshopper either, so few arrived, and still fewer remained, therefore each stranger was a curiosity. The difference was simply that those jet-eyed urchins were openly candid about it, and the men around town who'd also seen Anvil Wilson ride in, were more discreet.

Myer Frankel, the storekeeper, stood behind his fly-specked window with the local blacksmith, Jeff Stone, and speculated. "A cowboy," Myer said. "A bum. This time of year he should have a job down on the ranges, but he's one of them that can't keep from drifting. A saddlebum."

Myer was curly-headed and oily-skinned. No one would have believed it, but he had a very lucrative business at Grasshopper. Otherwise he never would have stayed because Myer was ambitious—or at least he had been ambitious when he'd arrived in Grasshopper twelve years before. He still was ambitious, but age and habit and solitude had made him also content. Nevertheless, unless he'd been making money he wouldn't have stayed.

That wasn't what kept Jeff Stone at Grasshopper. Jeff had come in six years before. He was a thick, burly man who feared neither man nor beast nor devil. But he did have a big and wholesome respect for the Apaches who lived all around Grasshopper, although there was little enough indication of this. Both Myer and Jeff were in their late forties.

So was Arch Pennington who owned Grasshopper's sole saloon, the *Trails End*. But everyone knew why Arch was in Grasshopper. He'd made the bad mistake of once holding up a stage containing the Territorial Governor. When an accused highwayman has as the prosecution's main witness against him the governor himself, he can begin estimating how old he'll be when he next sees free daylight. Arch had served his five years, and had come to Grasshopper right afterwards because he also liked seclusion.

Arch was a tight-lipped individual with hands like hams and eyes like chipped ice. The Indians respected him. So did the other whites around the countryside. Arch Pennington backed off for no man, red or white, and when he said something, whether it was a promise or a pronouncement, it was always truthful.

Arch came into Myer's store from the back way, went up where the other two were standing back from the window watching Anvil Wilson water his horse, and said, "I see you boys've already seen him." He got no reply to that, so he joined Jeff and Myer in watching Wilson. When the lanky stranger was bitting his horse again Arch said, "Now what; a lawman or an outlaw?"

Myer shrugged. "Leave it up to the deputy marshal either way. He's due to make his ride through sometime this week." Myer fished around under the counter, brought forth three crooked, bone-dry Mex cigars and placed them upon the countertop. He fished around for a soiled old checkerboard and laid that upon the countertop too. "He'll want shoes on his horse first," Myer said, up-ending a box of checkers, "So he'll go over to your shop, Jeff. Arch; you and I'll have time for two out of three before he either goes up to your place for a drink, or comes here to my place for grub."

Jeff stepped over, picked up one of the black little stogies, lit it and said, "Want to bet a dollar you're wrong, Myer?"

Before answering that Myer craned over to look out the window again. Anvil Wilson was standing over by the trough looking over the town. Myer leaned back eyeing Jeff.

"How—wrong?" he inquired.

"He's comin' in here first, and he's goin' to ask a lot of questions."

Myer continued to eye Jeff. Finally he said, "You know him; you know why he's in Grasshopper?"

"Yeah I know him," said Jeff. "I ought to know him." Jeff didn't enlarge upon that, but his expression was hard and calculating as he looked out the dirty window from between narrowed eyes, letting cigar smoke drift up past his face in the stale, utterly still air.

"Well . . ." said Myer, waiting.

"You'll find out soon enough," replied Jeff, and turned to walk out the back door.

Chapter Two

JEFF had been correct. Anvil led his animal over and made it fast to the hitch-rack out front of Myer's store, scuffed his feet to get the mud off his boots, acquired over at the leaking trough, and walked on into the hushed and shadowy general store. All he saw in there was a pair of men solemnly smoking and playing checkers.

The shelves were well-stocked, even down to glass mantles for coal-oil lamps, and cut plug. Flour barrels holding sugar, beans, even flour, lined one wall, their contents scrawled in crayon on the top of each barrel. There was one entire shelf of bolt goods, and across the large room securely locked inside a rickety glass case, were Colts pistols and Winchester carbines, time-honoured arbiters of all disputes in a land where legality rode with every man under the *rosadero* of his saddle, or strapped around his middle.

Anvil strolled over. Neither Arch nor Myer looked up right away, which would have been some kind of breach of decorum in Grasshopper, where nothing went unnoticed, but all the same everyone always pretended that it had, affecting a total indifference no one ever really felt.

Myer put down his stogie and, with both elbows planted upon his countertop, looked up. Anvil was softly smiling.

"You need supplies," said Myer, making a statement

of it. He waved one hand around. "I got it. You name it, mister; I got it."

Anvil's steady smile lingered. He dropped his glance to Pennington, who was closely studying Anvil through a cloud of bitter cigar smoke. Arch dropped his eyes to critically examine the length of ash on his Mex stogie, affecting that depthless indifference which fooled none of them.

"The supplies can come later," said Anvil. "What I'd like right now are some answers. I'm a stranger hereabouts. I need a place to bed down an' a place to fork feed to my horse."

"Help yourself," said Myer, gesturing again. "There are empty hogans around. As for feed – I got that out back. No hay, though, only grain. Barley and oats; a little cottoncake."

Anvil accepted this, paused a moment to glance over across the road where the little Indians were back playing in the mud again, then drifted his gaze southward along the row of warped and unpainted buildings as far as the smithy. "I need fresh shoes on my horse too," he murmured. "I see you got a forge in town."

"Yes," assented Myer, taking up his cigar again. "We also have a café, a harness shop, a saloon – this is Arch Pennington; he owns the saloon – and a strong jailhouse. We may be off the beaten track, mister, but we're not so far behind the times."

Anvil's grin lingered. His steady blue eyes behind the genial droop of lids, turned back to Myer and made a leisurely appraisal. "You also got a lot of mountains between you'n the rest of the world, and I like that, friend," he said.

Arch looked up again, curiosity showing brightly, but he said nothing. Arch was, along with being a fearless, truthful man, a fairly good judge of character. But this time he was stumped. In his secluded world strangers fell into one of two categories, providing they weren't Apaches: Lawman and outlawmen. The distinction was ordinarily not difficult to recognise, but this time it was. Bronzed, lanky, smiling Anvil Wilson could be either—or neither. He could have been, as a matter of fact, both at the same time, Arch smoked and speculated and felt gradually frustrated. It was annoying, after having so intimately associated with both kinds for five years down at the Territorial prison, not to be able to now figure out which this man was.

Myer looked out the window. "We have a good blacksmith. There's also a company of cavalry ten miles east, over at the town of White Mountain. And a deputy U.S. marshal over there named Carl Whitsett. In between there are the White Mountain Indians—Apaches." Myer looked back as he added: "Mexico's down across the mountains too."

Anvil said, "Thanks; I'll remember that." He seemed to be silently laughing at Myer for alternately warning him of the closeness of the law, and obliquely telling him how near he was to the Mex border in case he was on the dodge. "Right now I'd better get my horse shod. Later, I'll be back for some supplies."

He left the store, crossed over to his horse and led it back through the gelatin heatwaves to the blacksmith shop. Myer and Arch watched him through the store window. While they were doing that, another man came into Myer's building from out back. He moved with the total silence of an Indian and, because he wore Apache *n'deh b'keh* moccasins, got almost up to the front of the store before either Myer or Arch saw him. Arch swore, startled, and at the same time vexed at being caught spying on Anvil Wilson.

"Pat; when you goin' to quit wearin' them damned

Injun slippers? It's not seemly, a white man sneakin' around like that."

Pat was a grizzled, scarred man in his fifties, with an unshaven face and eyes that seemed never to remain still for more than a second or two. He was thick-shouldered and bandy-legged, built like a gorilla with hands that were strangely white and pulpy. "You try standin' on your feet all day like I do," he said with spirit, "and you'll find Injun slippers are a lot better'n cowhide boots. An' besides; what's the point of a feller who runs a café wearin' boots? My cowboy days was done with ten years back." Pat moved on up and craned towards the window, his voice and attitude changing. "So you fellers saw him too," he murmured. "Was he in here, Myer?"

"Yes."

"Well," demanded Pat, looking around.

Myer lifted and dropped his shoulders. He glanced at Arch as though passing the subject along. "He's a saddlebum by my guess. Arch . . . ?"

"More'n that," opined Pennington. "You saw how Jeff looked when he was in here, Myer. You heard what Jeff said about him."

"What did Jeff say?" Pat asked quickly. "He knew him?"

"He knew him," nodded Arch. "But you know Jeff—he could be tied to the tail of a wild horse and he wouldn't say a thing."

Pat leaned far over to look across the road again where Anvil Wilson was standing in the shade of the smithy, making a smoke and gazing up and down the roadway, while from deeper inside the sooty little shop the sounds of a struck anvil musically echoed.

"Lawman," pronounced Pat Culinan. "Lawman sure as I'm a foot tall."

"Or otherwise, maybe," muttered Myer, puffing on his little Mex stogie. "Who knows? One thing; he's new in the mountains."

"Another thing too," mumbled Arch. "He's poison. Look how he wears his forty-five an' how he keeps his back to the wall over there while he's lookin' us over. That smile don't fool me none. He's a gunfighter."

Pat asked: "What did he say his name was?"

"He didn't say. What's more I'm not goin' to ask," answered Arch, getting to his feet, hitching at his gunbelt, throwing a final long look over across the road. "I got to get back to the saloon," he announced, and walked back through the store, out into the back alley, and faded from sight.

The heat was a solid substance out in the roadway. It blanketed the entire broad clearing where Grasshopper stood with a leaden stillness. It moved when there was anything to make it move, like the ripples of an ocean. But because the people who lived here accepted it, never fought it, and moved almost as sluggishly as it also moved, there was nothing but stoic resignation about it.

Inside Jeff Stone's shop the sooty gloom made a kind of artificial shade, too. There was a barrel of water for cooling shoes fresh from the forge, as well as an olla hanging from a rafter, so the humidity in there made it more pleasant. Still, working over a cherry-red fire on such a day wasn't exactly anyone's idea of surcease. On the other hand, however, the White Mountains in wintertime got their share of bitterly cold weather. At that time of year the forge-fire was very welcome. A man couldn't expect everything; he had to take some discomfort in order to achieve some pleasure. In fact if there were no discomfort, how would he know what it was?

Jeff knew. He pumped his bellows and flung off sweat and worked with the sure, strong motions of an experienced smith. But all the time he was thinking the kind of thoughts that made a man uncomfortable, even without all that leaching heat.

When Anvil Wilson strolled back in out of the sunsmash to kill his cigarette in the water barrel and watch Jeff work, Stone was more acutely conscious of the lanky man's presence than he'd ever been with other strangers.

"Quiet town," said Anvil, genially, moving to make room as Jeff went past with the finished shoe and his nailing implements. "Ever have any trouble around here?"

"No," answered Jeff, bending to catch a foot and lift it. "Used to be Indian trouble, but that was before my time. Anyway, they got soldiers over at White Mountain." The shoe was a perfect fit. Jeff tossed aside his punch, hooked his farrier's hammer and rested the foot across his leg to start nailing.

"Get many strangers?" Anvil asked, idly watching the shoeing process.

"Not many," Jeff said tersely, and hammered in the first two nails before rearing back to critically examine the set and fit. "Now and then someone'll come through, but usually they don't stay. There's nothin' much here to keep a man."

"No cow outfits?"

"Not close by," Jeff retorted, bending to drive in the other six nails. "Westward there are some, but right around Grasshopper there aren't because it's Injun land. Oh; comes a drought-spring sometimes the cattlemen lease pasture up here and bring in herds, but that doesn't happen very often."

"Then it must be kind of dull," opined Anvil Wilson. "Work or drink—or maybe play checkers."

"We like it that way," answered Jeff, clinching the nails, groping for his rasp to level the clinches and smooth the outside hoof. "The folks here in Grasshopper don't like cities or crowds, mister, otherwise they wouldn't be livin' here." Jeff dropped the last hoof, straightened up, winced from a little jab of pain in his back and flung off sweat. He looked squarely at Anvil Wilson, then stepped past to shed his mule-skin apron, fling his hand-tools in the bucket reserved for them, and plunge both arms half way to the shoulders in the water barrel. He was finished. Wilson's big sorrel horse was well shod all around. "That'll be one dollar," he said, stepping back from the water barrel.

The dollar was handed over. Jeff stonily regarded it a moment, clearly balancing some thought in his mind. "If you're lookin' for someone," he eventually said, his words slow and toneless, "you're wastin' your time, mister. The folks who know where Grasshopper is, either come here because they live hereabouts, or they don't come here because there's soldiers and a deputy U.S. marshal at the next town." He pocketed the silver cartwheel and raised his flinty stare. "That's about the size of it."

Anvil Wilson, in the act of lowering his stirrups where they'd been tied over the saddlehorn to keep from hitting the blacksmith's head while he worked, completed that chore with leisurely movements, and finally turned to regard Jeff Stone with fresh, unsmiling interest.

"You know me, don't you?" he said.

Jeff nodded. "I know you, mister. I don't know your name, but I know you. You're the man from Cody County. I heard you called that down at Tucson one time, years back."

Anvil still didn't smile. His blue gaze lay unwaveringly upon the blacksmith. "You have a good memory," he murmured. "Now what, blacksmith; run across the road and tell the others?"

"No," Jeff replied quietly. "They can find out for themselves. They're not in trouble an' neither am I, mister. I've been minding my own business for a long time. Most of my life. I'll go right on minding it."

Anvil led his horse over near the doorway and stopped to stand in the shade a moment longer while he made a sceptical assessment of Jeff Stone. "That means you wouldn't tell me anything either, doesn't it?" he asked.

"It does. Like I said, I mind my own business. I'm a blacksmith an' that's all I am. Fellers like you mean trouble. I've already told you there's nothing here in Grasshopper. You won't hang around long." Jeff removed his shoeing apron and tossed it aside. He started across towards the doorway as though to walk on out. Anvil Wilson didn't budge an inch. He blocked the exit.

"Blacksmith," he said, when they were face to face, "I sure hope you're a man of your word. You don't answer questions for me; you don't answer them for that storekeeper over there, or the saloonman." Anvil smiled. "You an' I are goin' to get along right well." He moved his horse enough to let Jeff walk out into the dusty roadway. He let Jeff get twenty feet on his way before he called after him, saying, "I'll be around for a few days, blacksmith. If you're up at the saloon maybe we can share a drink."

Anvil's next occupation, after seeing that his horse was fresh-shod and ready to go, was to locate a hogan that didn't have a sunken floor, a den of rattlers in it, or wasn't too otherwise inhabited by crawling critters. He found the one he wanted north of Grasshopper where the trail through town branched off, one side heading for the westerly, lower and grassy slopes, the other side striking out straight for the bluish mountains.

There was horse feed out there, too, where he hobbled his big sorrel horse, and nearby was a little branching segment of the livelier watercourse that ran down behind town. Altogether, after he routed the larger critters from within his brush-shelter, his living accommodations weren't too bad. Of course, after sunset, there would be mosquitoes, but if a man built a little smoky fire they wouldn't get too much of his blood.

Then Anvil Wilson settled down to wait.

So did Grasshopper; it wondered about him, speculated, argued, tried to draw Jeff out, failed, and garrulously, ceaselessly pondered on this fresh presence of a smiling, hard-eyed, lanky gunfighter, for no one doubted at all but that was what Anvil Wilson was.

Chapter Three

JOHN WEST ran a few cows in the lower, westerly foothills. John also had a little crevice-mine where he
flaked out a dollar a day, sometimes, weather and John's
rheumatism permitting. He was in his sixties he said,
but Myer and Arch and Pat Culinan swore up and
down he'd been in the Grasshopper country nearly twice
that long. There were old Apache bucks who would
grin like imps, showing toothless gums and wizened,
parchment faces, when anyone said John West was
middle-aged. But it was Apache custom to keep private
the things which men shared, and old John West's age
seemed to be one of those private matters.

Upon the few occasions each year that John visited
Myer's store, he always paid with gold dust. Sometimes
he had a pea-sized nugget or two. It was rumoured that
John had been married twice. Once to a buxom white
woman, once to a buxom squaw. But since John never
mentioned it, and no one had the gall to come right out
and ask, there was no actual proof that John had been
married. Certainly he was not married now; he lived
out there atop his low hill in an old adobe house the
army had built many years back as a sort of outpost.
John hadn't done anything to the house, but he had
built a fine log barn. It had taken him four years to do
it, but in the White Mountains no one valued time very
much. He had his few head of cows, his crevice-mine,
and about twenty head of very excellent steeldust horses.

Old John was a regular fanatic about horses. He'd no more ride a mare than he'd have moved into a hogan. He got along with the Indians, but he made no secret of the fact that he mostly held them in deep contempt.

Not because they were mean or dirty or even treacherous, but rather, as he'd once confided in Arch Pennington after he'd been drinking most of the day, because they'd allowed the whites to take everything away from them.

"A man's better off dead," he snarled, "than livin' off gov'ment bounty. If they'd had the sense God give a woodtick they'd have fought right down to the last pinch of powder. Now look at 'em; out there in the lousy mountains livin' like animals."

Arch had suggested the Apaches had always lived like animals. That, in fact, they *enjoyed* living like animals.

That brought a roar from old John and a flash of latent fire into his piercing, faded old smoky eyes. "That's all you know about it," he'd sworn, hammering the bartop with a gnarled old fist. "They got feelings too."

Arch hadn't cared, actually, but he'd been stung, so he'd said, "So have the Mexicans," meaning that what everyone knew still went on—Apache raids down into Mexico—caused deaths and wails and anguish below the line.

But John'd had his answer to that. He had stiffly drawn himself very erect, and looked down his long, hooked nose at Arch. "In case you didn't know," he'd pronounced, making a point of enunciating very clearly. "Apaches been raidin' Mexico for hundreds of years. It's their right; just like it's your right to go huntin' in the mountains, an' just like it's my right to quit drinkin' in this pig sty!"

And that had been the last time old John had stepped foot inside Arch's *Trails End* Saloon, which didn't harm

Arch very much but it played old nick with John, because no one else in Grasshopper stocked raw spirits, of which old John was very fond.

That's why John sat down upon the roadside bench in front of Myer's store, beside Anvil Wilson, when he rode into town and spied a genuine-enough stranger, because John was a man of high principle. He wanted a drink so bad his throat felt like parchment, but he'd have withered and died before he'd have poked his big hooked nose inside Arch's doorway.

"Don't get many travellers hereabouts," he said genially, squinting around at the equally as lanky, rawboned man. "My name's John West. I got a place westerly a piece."

Anvil said his own name and exchanged old John's look of frank interest. He suspected how it was with old John so he said, grinning, "Come on up an' join me in a drink at the saloon, Mister West."

The answer came swiftly. "Oh no, Mister Wilson. No, I couldn't do that. But was you to fetch a bottle back down here, why I'd be mighty proud to set with you."

Over across the road in his shop, Jeff Stone heard Anvil's booming laugh. So did Myer, who was behind his counter making up an order for some hunters who'd passed through right at sunup and who'd return in another three or four days on their way back down out of the mountains. Even Pat Culinan heard it, but he'd have heard it anyway because Pat had taken a fierce interest in Anvil Wilson and made a special point of spying on him from across the road inside his dingy little cubbyhole café.

The man who didn't hear Anvil's laugh was Arch Pennington up at his saloon, but at least he capitalised from it and none of the others did. Arch sold Anvil a quart of tequila, with a bloated dead worm in the bottle to attest its quality, and didn't know what Wilson had in mind to do with all that liquor until he went out a half hour later to sweep the walkway in front of the saloon. Then he made a sniffing sound of strong disdain at the sight of John West down there in the shade on that bench drinking Anvil Wilson's liquor.

But it was a dollar well spent, in Anvil's view. John West knew the White Mountains as well as any Apache and far better than any white man then alive. The more of that tequila he drank the more exclamatory he became, but it was interesting. Anvil sat there taking an occasional stingy sip, his hatbrim tilted low to shield his eyes, one leg hooked over the other one, listening. He learned the names of canyons and plateaux and peaks which would have defied any interpreter because they were names cobbled together by white men who understood border-Spanish and reservation-Apache, making a tongue-twisting combination which had meaning only for very few hard-bitten old renegades, long gone and forgotten.

He heard of the different clans and where they camped in the mountains. Finally, it came out in bitter tones why old John West wouldn't enter Pennington's saloon. Then, as John arose to set a steady course for his patient horse out there in the hot afternoon, he told Anvil Wilson for the third time how to reach his ranch, got aboard, turned and with considerable dignity rode back up the thoroughfare northward bound out of Grasshopper, entirely forgetting that he'd ridden in to buy staples.

Anvil Wilson had an empty bottle and a world of excellent background information about the White Mountains, all for one silver cartwheel: a genuine bargain.

He sauntered over to Culinan's café and had dinner—

which was the noon-day meal in cow country. The last meal of the day was called supper. Pat was right there with a pithy comment.

"Mister; I seen you over there listenin' to John West. Well sir; he's an old renegade. They say he even used to go on raids with the 'Paches. There's more'n one grisly story of him ambushin' Mex soldiers to let those thievin' rascals get over the line before the greasers caught 'em. He even had a squaw one time, what d'you think of that?"

Anvil leaned far over the lunch counter and gazed floorward without saying a word. Pat got red in the face. Everyone seemed to make a particular point of observing that he wore Apache slippers and it was exasperating.

"I got bunions," he waspishly snapped. "Besides, I'm on my feet all day."

Anvil smiled and held aloft his coffee cup for a re-fill. He kept right on smiling all the while Pat was filling the cup.

In a place like Grasshopper, Arizona Territory, time hung heavy even for those with something to do. For a man like lanky Anvil Wilson it should have driven him to drink, sitting on that bench out front of Myer's place every day, sometimes whittling on a stick, sometimes tilting down his hatbrim for a little nap, sometimes slouching there as motionless as stone studying cloud-shadows over the mountains, or watching how the sun burned its midsummer way up and down the tilted land.

"He's got to be waitin' for someone," Arch Pennington told Myer the third day, as they played two out of three at the checkerboard.

"Waiting?" Myer murmured. "What would a man like him be waiting for in Grasshopper? What happens

here that could interest him? The mail packer'll be
through day after tomorrow. Marshal Whitsett's due
maybe next week. Two months from now the Indians'll
start coming to trade, their summer hunt finished. What
among all that would interest a man like this Anvil
Wilson?"

Pat had a tart reply. "Ask Jeff, he'd know. Your
move."

But Jeff kept his word. He visited evenings with the
others upon the porch of Culinan's place, or he bought
a round of tepid ale up at Arch's saloon. But when those
pointed little hints were dropped, he completely ignored
them.

The man who packed in mail and small packages for
Grasshopper lived over at Hereford, another White
Mountain community. He'd been making that trip
seven years, and as he later told Marshal Whitsett when
they met over at White Mountain, in all those seven
years he hadn't seen but four or five strangers at Grasshopper who weren't just passing through.

Carl Whitsett was interested. The scourge of his
existence were shadowy individuals who showed up in
the mountains near the end of every summer to barter
and buy outright, whatever trinkets the Apaches had
smuggled back out of Mexico. Except for these men,
Whitsett's superiors often said, the raiding trips down
into Mexico wouldn't be lucrative enough to interest
renegade Indians.

That was pure bunk. Apaches didn't raid for the gold
rings and necklaces they tore from the bodies of their
murdered victims. They raided for the sheer love of
being marauders. They'd been doing it for a thousand
years, more or less, one place or another; they weren't
corn-planters or great hunters, they were reavers—
people who made a career out of being Huns. That was

their history; it was also their pride and joy. But now they were very sly about it because the U.S. Army, and the U.S. Marshal's office down at Tucson, were adamantly opposed to it. That didn't stop the bolder bucks from raiding, but it surely made Carl Whitsett's job harder.

He thought Anvil Wilson was one of those gold-buyers, which is why he rode over to Grasshopper. But the day he arrived there some cowboys from below the westward slopes drifted in a herd of critters for mid-summer grazing, and when Carl arrived in town the cowboys were whooping it up and there was no sign of Anvil Wilson.

"Damned if I know," Arch Pennington told Marshal Whitsett, over the racket of those rangeriders noisily drinking and gambling at the *Trails End*. "Every day since he come here he's sat down there in front of Myer's place snoozin' in the sun or whittlin' little wooden horses out of pieces of wood. If he's not down there today, maybe Myer'd know what become of him. As you can see, I haven't had much time to be outside today."

Whitsett went down to the general store. He was a youngish man, in his thirties somewhere, tall and lean and blue-eyed, shrewd and tough and resourceful. He'd weathered his share of life's crises, and it showed in the way he handled himself. He was a thoughtful, steady man, bony-fisted and gun-handy. Over at White Mountain where they had a town marshal, Carl Whitsett was one man the tough element of border-jumpers mightily respected. He was said to be as fast with a gun as any man in Arizona, which was saying quite a lot; Arizona, with its convenient access to Mexico, was notorious for the number and variety of its nightriders.

But Myer knew nothing. All he could say for a fact was that the bench Wilson usually occupied was empty.

But Myer made a suggestion. "Go see Jeff over at the shoeing shop. He knows something about this Anvil Wilson."

"What does he know?" Whitsett asked.

Myer shrugged. "He hasn't told any of us around Grasshopper, but maybe he'll tell you."

It was a poor guess. Jeff stonily listened to Marshal Whitsett and remained unmoved. "I saw him down south a time or two," he explained. "But I never had dealings with him until I shod his horse the day he arrived here, last week. Beyond that I'm not interested in him, and he's not interested in me. I'm content to have it that way, Marshal."

Whitsett went up to Pat's café for his dinner. There were three of those lowland cowboys up there also wolfing down Pat's beans and fried steak. Marshal Whitsett sat and waited and sipped coffee. He had more time than the cowboys did. He had a particular old brush shelter where he oftentimes spent the night, when duty brought him to Grasshopper. The cowboys finally left, heading straight back across the road to the *Trails End*, spurs ringing, voices loud and rough. Finally, Carl asked Pat about Anvil Wilson.

Pat was busy piling dirty dishes, but he left that to draw up a stool across the bench and say in a low, conspiratorial tone of voice, "Marshal, I'm plumb glad you asked. No; I got no idea where he went this morning, but I can tell you he's a bad one. Now then, I've lived better'n fifty years, an' I've seen my share of gunmen, you realise, so when this Wilson come into town on that big sorrel geldin' of his'n, I said to myself I said: Pat; there's a killer."

Marshal Whitsett sighed, gulped down the last of his coffee, dropped a nickel on the counter and stood up. "I'm obliged for your help, Pat," he said. "Reckon I'll go make camp and wait around for Wilson to come back."

Back out in the fading light of late afternoon Carl Whitsett watched the lowland rangeriders troop out of Pennington's saloon to their horses, somewhat unsteady on their feet. He didn't know the riders but he knew the outfit they rode for. It was the Flying R ranch thirty miles southwest below the foothills.

The rangemen whirled and dashed down through Grasshopper stirring up a mighty dust. Marshal Whitsett waited a moment to let it settle, then strode over where his horse was tied, got the animal and led it northward beyond town where that hogan was he used on his over-night trips to the Grasshopper county. He didn't like staying all night but if he wished to see Anvil Wilson he obviously was going to have to. Every man's occupation has some particular facet he doesn't like. Sleeping in abandoned old spider-infested hogans was Carl Whitsett's disagreeable obligation.

Chapter Four

ANOTHER element of his job Carl didn't like was the waiting. He therefore had two reasons for feeling disgruntled. After a miserable night in the old hogan he waited around town all the following day, and Anvil Wilson never showed up.

He went out to the hogan Wilson had used, ascertained from the few meagre belongings left there that Wilson meant to return, and stubbornly went back to Pat's café for his meals. He meant to wait Wilson out, now, if it took a week.

But they didn't meet.

The second day a mounted soldier rode over to Grasshopper from White Mountain with a message for Marshal Whitsett from his commanding officer, and Carl had struck his camp, saddled up and departed, with the soldier.

One hour later Anvil Wilson walked his horse into town from the north, looking fresh and amiable and satisfied.

That evening when Jeff and Myer and Pat got together over at Arch's saloon, the consensus was that Wilson had shown up too soon after Whitsett's departure.

"He knew," Pat emphatically stated. "He knew Carl was here. He was probably lyin' back up there in the northward forest with a spyglass or something, watchin'."

That seemed plausible, but it also deepened the

mystery. There unquestionably would have been more of this type of speculation, but Anvil himself entered the saloon, killing all further such talk with his presence.

Still, the others had their private reflections, which ran along similar lines, with the upshoot being that Anvil Wilson was watching the town. It shook them a little; made them act guilty whether they felt that way or not. Only Jeff remained largely aloof. He couldn't of course entirely divorce himself from what was going on; Grasshopper was much too small for that, but he nevertheless refused to be drawn into any of those furtive discussions. The inevitable result of his attitude was that the others began viewing Jeff with some doubt and suspicion.

"What's he so damned secretive about?" Arch asked the others, one night when Wilson hadn't yet appeared at the saloon for his usual nightcap. "If he's scairt of Wilson, why don't he slip over to White Mountain and tell Whitsett what's on his mind?"

There was several answers to that, of course, so no one felt impelled to reply, but one thing became prominently obvious as the days passed. The men of Grasshopper were beginning to change. Not only towards one another, but also towards Jeff Stone.

When those hunters returned from the mountains to pick up their purchases at Myer's store, it offered a brief diversion. There were three of those strangers, all range-riders and all rough-looking men.

It was a little early for hunting, actually; the bucks and other upland game weren't really prime until after the first frost, usually sometime in early September. Still, hunters sometimes preferred the warmer weather so no one was much concerned.

The biggest man among that trio was a black-eyed, black-bearded, shaggy-headed individual who had shoulders like an ox and a fist like a granite boulder. He said his name was Pert Fox. His friends were named Cap Beeson and Wes Hall. Both Beeson and Hall were somewhat younger than Pert Fox, and seemed to go pretty much on what Pert Fox said. At the saloon they let it be known the hunting had been lousy.

"Too hot up there," Fox had boomed, calling on Arch to set up drinks for the house. "Too early in the season, I reckon. The deer are still higher up near the snowfields, maybe, but wherever they are, we can tell you for a fact they ain't down low enough to get at 'em yet."

Jeff lifted his glass. "Better luck next time," he said.

Pat Culinan, after his third drink, was full of sage advice about hunting in the White Mountains. Arch knew the only way to shut him up and proceeded to do it; he set up one drink right after another until Pat's tongue got so thick, his legs so unsteady, that he dissolved into a corner and fell pleasantly asleep. He'd be mad at himself in the morning and he'd darkly suspect what Arch had done to him, but that would be the end of it.

The hunters lay over a day, loafing and spinning tales of great hunts they'd been on up at the saloon. If they knew Anvil Wilson was around they didn't mention it, but more than likely they had no idea because Anvil disappeared the day they came down into town, the same way he'd disappeared the day Carl Whitsett had come to Grasshopper. Furthermore, Anvil stayed away just as long the second time as he had that first time.

The hunters chided Pat about having a headache, while eating over at his café, and laughed at his forlorn expression. They picked up their supplies from Myer and packed out the morning of the third day, leaving behind a pleasant little aura, for they'd spent close to a hundred dollars in Grasshopper.

That evening Anvil rode in, put up his horse and had supper at Pat's café before ambling on over to the saloon for a few drinks.

"Something damned funny goin' on here," Arch confided in Myer, before he went on down his bar to serve Anvil. Myer drank his ale, studied Pennington's backbar, and solitarily savoured the pleasant sensation of alcohol loosening all his inherent inhibitions. In this life, he mused, there was usually something "damned funny" going on wherever humanity congregated. A wise man kept clear, took his profit, and tried somehow to lay enough by for his old age. Beyond that, in a place like Grasshopper, what else was there to be done?

Anvil bought one round for the others and paid for it with a little rough nugget of raw gold. Arch picked up the nugget and squinted at it. "You get lucky?" he asked Anvil. "Not much of this stuff left around to be picked up any more."

"Won it in a poker game," explained Anvil.

Arch lifted his eyes. Only one man still scratched out gold; John West. He hefted the pebble, speculating about that.

"Isn't it enough?" Anvil inquired.

"Sure," nodded Arch. "It's enough for the second round too."

"Then set 'em up all around because I've got a couple more," replied Wilson, smiling quietly at Arch.

Arch complied. The others accepted their free drinks and stood along the bar eyeing that little golden pebble where Arch put it down for them all to see, his purpose very clear. Anvil Wilson was spending some of the time he wasted away from town, down at old John West's place. That opened up a whole new vista for speculation.

After his second drink Pat Culinan sidled over to

Wilson and said, "You're not a card-shark, are you, pardner?" and when Anvil replied that he was not, Pat invited him to a game of two-handed draw poker.

Jeff was absent from the saloon that evening but the others ignored that fact. They had turned decidedly cool towards Jeff lately.

Myer, who never gambled, drew up a chair and watched the poker game. Arch and his gold nugget kept company over at the bar. There was something about gold, even tiny pebbles of it, that did things to men.

Pat had passed his three-drink limit and wasn't playing good cards. Still; he won for a while, until, between fuzzy thinking and clumsy card-handling, Lady Luck turned on him. After that Anvil Wilson won Pat's three silver cartwheels, all he had on him, and after that the game seesawed back and forth with meals over at Pat's café as Culinan's share of each pot.

It was close to ten o'clock when Jeff walked in looking tired and thirsty. Arch poured him a drink and pocketed his nugget. He and Myer settled their attention upon Stone for a curious moment, then lost interest as Jeff sauntered over to also watch the card game. He eventually bought in, and after that Anvil's luck began changing. Jeff played poker like he did most other things; quietly, thoughtfully, and grimly.

An hour later Marshal Carl Whitsett came into the saloon. Arch and the others were surprised and showed it. None of them could recall ever having seen Carl appear in Grasshopper after sundown before.

Carl nodded around and bellied up to the bar for a drink. He and Anvil Wilson exchanged a solemn nod but that was all.

Wilson's little faint smile gradually died out altogether. Once or twice he glanced across the table at Jeff, his blue eyes mirroring some scepticism. Pat Culinan got sleepy and dropped out of the game. It was perhaps just as well because he owed Anvil Wilson six meals. Pat padded soundlessly over to the bar and slapped down his pulpy paw.

"One for the road," he said to Arch. "I'll pay you tomorrow."

"Sure," growled Arch, and fished around under his bar a moment, brought forth a cup of black, hot coffee, and placed it squarely in front of Culinan. Pat recoiled as though a rattlesnake had suddenly appeared upon the bartop. Carl Whitsett grinned. Myer smiled too. Jeff Stone, glancing over, chuckled.

"Now what the hell," demanded Pat, raising indignant eyes, "is the meanin' o' this, Arch Pennington. I asked for a drink—not this stuff. Look at it; black as your blasted heart and hot enough to melt the ears off'n a brass monkey."

"It's on the house," Arch calmly replied. "Pat; in the mornin' you'll thank me."

"Well in that case," exclaimed Culinan, "wait until the mornin' to give it to me. Right now, what I want is a shot of rye whisky or tequila."

He got his rye whisky and he drank it, then he turned and hitched up his trousers, studied the exact location of the yonder doorway, squared his shoulders and started rolling ahead. Everyone watched him, even Anvil Wilson and Jeff Stone at their card table. Some of the undercurrent which had come into the saloon along with Marshal Whitsett, atrophied, which made it easier for the others to relax and smile a little.

Pat cleared the door with ample room and passed from sight. Then, five seconds later, they all heard him miss the step from the plankwalk out into the roadway, and crash to earth with a mighty curse and a howl.

"They got me, boys," he bellowed, fiercely thrashing

out there in the moonlighted roadway. "Leggo me ye dirty h'athens; take ye're murderin' hands off me!"

Arch came from behind his bar with a look of exasperation and headed for the doorway. As an explanation he said, "The darned old idiot'll be fightin' 'Paches up an' down the roadway all night unless someone sees him over to bed. I've seen him do it before."

Myer lifted his shoulders and dropped them. "It's true," he told Anvil. "Pat's a man who can't handle liquor."

Jeff cashed in and got up to leave. As he did so Anvil put a quiet look upwards at him. "It's a smart man who knows when to quit," he said, an obvious double meaning to his words.

He and Jeff exchanged a look, then the blacksmith turned and also walked out of the saloon. That left a chair vacant at the card table, which Marshal Whitsett strolled over and occupied. He and Anvil eyed each other, then Wilson picked up the cards and began shuffling them. When he flipped the first pasteboard over in front of the lawman, Whitsett shook his head. "Let's just talk a little," he said. "I was here a week or so back and missed you. I'm Deputy U.S. Marshal Carl Whitsett from over at White Mountain."

Anvil lay the cards aside. "Wilson," he murmured. "Anvil Wilson, Marshal, from a lot of different places."

"Yeah I know," stated Carl, leaning back in his chair. "I heard you used to hang out down around Tucson, Anvil. I talked to some rangemen who knew you over at Tombstone, also."

Anvil picked up the cards again without speaking and began making a solitaire layout. He studied each card as he placed it face-up in front of him. He obviously was going to make Whitsett carry the full burden of their conversation. He didn't seem hostile, just cold towards Carl.

Whitsett waited a moment to be sure that Anvil wanted it this way, then he said, "I'm interested in what you're doing over here at Grasshopper, Anvil."

"Didn't the blacksmith have that figured out?" Anvil retorted.

"For the record, Anvil," stated Marshal Whitsett, "Jeff Stone didn't fetch me. I came on my own."

"Odd," murmured Anvil, bending forward a little to gaze at his solitaire hand. "He's been gone from town most of the day, which would've given him plenty of time to ride over to White Mountain and back again."

"I'll tell you again," repeated Carl. "Stone didn't come after me. I came over on my own."

Arch stamped back into the saloon looking annoyed, but by the time he'd gotten back behind his bar once more, he caught the turbulence in the atmosphere and raised his eyebrows at Myer, who walked over to have another ale, ostensibly, but actually because Myer smelled trouble coming and didn't want to be around that card table when it arrived.

But the varieties of trouble, like the varieties of men, are endless, what seemed like trouble to Myer Frankel to whom anything disagreeable was trouble, was nothing more, evidently, to the pair of men over at that card table, than some verbal fencing and some give and take.

"Let's leave Stone out of it," said Carl Whitsett, then paused to look sharply where Anvil Wilson turned up a face-card. "Play the Queen on your red King," he said.

Anvil paused, raised his eyes, and grinned. It wasn't that quiet, easy smile of his, it was instead a grin of candid amusement. He played the Queen on the red King, tossed down the cards and called out:

"Barman; fetch over a bottle and two glasses."

That ended the trouble, or at least the outward signs of trouble. Arch brought over the bottle and glasses, then retreated. Myer put a silver coin atop the bar and departed, grateful for the opportunity to do so and still convinced there would be trouble. He was right, of course, but not at that particular time or place.

Chapter Five

ARCH didn't hear what was said between Marshal Whitsett and lanky Anvil Wilson. Partly because, as they drank and talked, they spoke in quiet-calm tones, but also because, after a couple of drinks they strolled outside where the moonlight lay in soft layers over the mountains, the village, and the pair of tall men.

Arch tried though; he even went over to the door and peered out, but the lawman and Anvil Wilson were walking slowly down the bland night in the direction of the log jailhouse.

That was the last Arch saw of them together that night. The next morning when Pat Culinan came over to shakily demand a dram of the hair of the dog that had bitten him the evening before, Arch morosely reported what he'd seen and heard, but Pat wasn't interested until after his third straight shot, and by then Jeff Stone came up to ask whether Pat intended to drink himself to death at Arch's place, or get his spindly shanks across the road and get dinner for a working blacksmith. Pat retreated, but not in very good humour.

An odd thing happened that day. Right after Carl Whitsett rode out of Grasshopper three riders appeared out along a westerly ridge in plain sight, watching the town. Arch saw them. So did Myer Frankel, who was coming back from Pat's café when they appeared out there. He called over to Jeff to look, and the blacksmith also saw them.

Anvil didn't, though, because he wasn't in his usual

place outside Myer's store on the wall-bench. He wasn't even in town, as a matter of fact, and he didn't get back to town until midafternoon, by which time those three mysterious horsemen had long since disappeared.

That evening another odd thing happened. A squad of soldiers rattled into town looking dusty and droopy from the heat. Their sergeant was a red-necked Irishman with a bullet-shaped head and a garrulous, gravel-like voice. The soldiers set up camp out behind town at the creek and except for the sergeant didn't walk over among the buildings. Arch sold the red-necked non-com. a bottle of hard liquor and tried to elicit some information. All Arch got was an antagonistic stare and an oath about the high cost of whisky at Grasshopper.

Myer, when Arch related all this to him, said with a sage look, "I knew it. I felt trouble coming last night when Whitsett walked in. Why soldiers, I'd like to know?"

The word spread fast, too. Jeff and Pat showed up at Myer's store to verify what was happening, then they walked out back and gazed over beside the creek where that squad of men in blue uniforms were bivouacing.

"It's like Myer says," averred Pat morosely. "Something's afoot."

Anvil returned to town in early evening and for once he had no hint of a smile upon his bronzed features. He cared for his sorrel horse, went up to the saloon, sat down and told Arch to fetch him some ale. He sat and drank and ignored the others as they drifted in as usual, one at a time, just after sunset. The soldiers never did come around. Pat Culinan went out to see whether or not they were still there.

They were, but by dawn they weren't, and that started the uneasiness up all over again. But at least this day Anvil remained in town. He went back to his earlier pastime of sitting out front of Myer's store, whittling.

That same morning old John West came to town, his second trip in two weeks, which was noteworthy in itself, but what was more noteworthy was the fact that old John tied up out front of Myer's place, went over and whispered something to Anvil Wilson, and afterwards walked into the store to buy some tinned goods, some flour and sugar—and several boxes of carbine and beltgun ammunition.

Myer said, "Going hunting?"

Old John replied enigmatically. "You could call it that, I expect, but I'd be more inclined to say I was goin' protectin'."

When Myer tried to get some sense out of the old man, Anvil appeared in his doorway, slouching there, looking and listening. Myer desisted and went about his chores.

For a half hour after that old John and Anvil Wilson sat out there mumbling occasionally back and forth on Anvil's bench before John loaded his animal, clambered back astride and rode on out of town without even turning his head as he passed Arch's saloon.

"It's the lousy heat," complained Pat, sober but shaky, the day after John West had appeared in town. He told that to Jeff down at the blacksmith shop. "Heat makes folks think an' do foolish things."

Jeff had a comment about that. "The heat doesn't make soldiers ride into the mountains in squad strength, Pat."

Culinan raised his eyebrows. "Is that where the soljers went?"

"It is. I rode over to the creek looking for salt an' saw their tracks as plain as day. U.S. calks on their horses heading straight up into the mountains."

"Injun trouble more'n likely," opined Pat, after a moment's concentration. "The gold buyers probably took 'em in some likker. I tell you, Jeff, likker's the downfall of mankind." Pat padded back up towards his café after making that philosophical observation, and Jeff Stone moved over to the door of his shop to see where Anvil Wilson was.

Anvil was sitting loose and easy over on his bench whittling out a fine steeldust horse from a piece of white pine. If one man's attitude could possibly reflect the attitude of a town, Anvil's would have proclaimed to the world that all was well in Grasshopper, which would have been the most incorrect syllepsis of all time, but for another day no one around Grasshopper would be certain of that.

The troopers did not return that day. Nothing else of interest broke the monotonously dull pattern of Grasshopper's social existence until just before sunset. Then Pert Fox appeared in town all by himself without any warning at all.

He went to Arch's saloon, had two quick ones, then walked over to the doorway to study the shimmering little town with his third drink in hand. Finally, he went back to the bar, leaned across it and fixed Arch with his black, hard stare, and said, "Barman; you had any strangers around here the last day or two?"

Arch thought of Anvil, but he was hardly a stranger any longer. He also recalled the soldiers, but they weren't exactly strangers either, so he shook his head at big Pert, wondering privately what had brought the hunter back to Grasshopper.

"No; none that I saw anyway, Mister Fox. Why?"

Fox didn't answer. He considered Arch a long time, had one more drink, then left the saloon, got on his horse and rode back westerly out of town again.

When they all met as usual that late evening Arch related what he knew of the visit of Pert Fox. Jeff Stone, accepted back into the confidence of his friends again because they privately thought he'd gone after Carl Whitsett the other night, and was therefore on their side after all, put two and two together and came up with a suggestion.

"Fox had two other fellers hunting with him. Those fellers sitting out there to the west today watching the town, were three in number."

Myer thought about that a moment then said, "But why? Those men were hunters. They'd been into the mountains. When they came back they bought supplies from me on their way out."

"What of that?" argued Jeff. "They went out a ways and made their camp. They've got the supplies to live off of. But if they were hunters and the huntin' was as lousy as they said—what're they hangin' around here for?"

Arch and Pat pondered this exchange in long silence. Finally Pat perked up and said, "Where's Wilson? How come him not to be in yet for his nightcap?"

Before anyone could reply they all distinctly heard a horseman coming down the hushed roadway from the north. "There's your answer," Arch said to Pat. "He's comin' now."

But Pat was badly in error. The rider stopped outside, all right, they all heard him do that. They also heard him get down from his saddle, but after that there was a long delay before he got around to the plankwalk, and began shuffling across it. Arch put a glass on the bar, poured it full of Anvil Wilson's favourite whisky, and froze there with the upraised bottle in his hand, his bulging eyes locked upon the yonder doorway.

That red-faced sergeant of troopers came half way into the room, clinging to both Arch's batwing-doors, his face drained and grey, his eyes out of focus, his blue blouse caked with drying blood, then he collapsed, falling into the saloon with a shuddering crash.

For a moment no one moved or seemed to even breathe. Myer sat there, stunned. Pat Culinan tried to swallow and couldn't. Jeff turned all the way around against the bar, hung there for several seconds, then pushed off to cross over and look down.

"Shot," he exclaimed in a strained voice. "He's been shot. Arch; fetch him some whisky. Pat, help me straighten him out."

Gradually, as the shock passed, they began moving, began doing what they could for the injured soldier. Arch got the liquor past the sergeant's lips, but it spilled back out again. Myer went after some water while Pat and Jeff arranged the sergeant's limbs.

That's when Anvil Wilson came up out of the roadway's darkness and halted to watch. For a while he simply looked on, the others heedless of his presence, then Anvil knelt, lifted the sergeant's head so that Arch could try getting another shot poured down, and when that also ran back out Anvil bent in the guttery lamplight for a close look, and gently put the sergeant back down as he said, "No use; he's dead."

They were appalled. They'd all seen death before, even this kind of violent death, but since there seemed absolutely no explanation for it here and now, they were left hanging.

Anvil got up, stepped back outside and looked the length of the roadway. For a while he remained like that. Arch and Jeff came out to join in after a few moments.

"Where are they?" murmured Arch, squinting into darkness. "There was a full squad of 'em."

"Not coming," said Anvil, relaxing, turning to gaze back inside where the doors hung open.

"Sure they're coming," mumbled Arch, unwilling to believe this tragedy could be any greater than it already was. "Hell man, there were eight of 'em. They didn't *all* get shot."

"No?" murmured Anvil. "I wonder about that."

Jeff stared. So did Arch and Myer and Pat. They regarded Anvil Wilson as though he'd just made a statement that took away their breath.

Anvil knelt and rummaged through the dead sergeant's pockets. The others drew aside, shocked and a little suspicious about that. But all Anvil turned up were some personal belongings; a Barlow clasp knife, some coins, a gnawed plug of chewing tobacco, a stub of a pencil and a little notebook. Anvil went over under the lamp to look through the notebook, but it evidently held nothing that interested him because he went back and handed the book to Arch.

"Put all his stuff together," Anvil said crisply. "Keep it until Whitsett or the military come over here."

Anvil left the saloon, walking briskly. It was then about nine o'clock. Arch gathered up the dead soldier's effects, tied them in a little bundle using the sergeant's own neckerchief for this purpose, went back around his bar and poured himself a double shot.

The others drew away, leaving that dead man lying. All manner of thoughts assailed them. "Injuns," whispered Pat Culinan. "Sure as the devil the 'Paches done that. Wiped out the whole squad of 'em."

"You're talkin' through your hat," muttered Jeff Stone, also crossing back to the bar for a stiff one. But Jeff's words didn't quite carry the conviction they should have. "Pour me a double one too," he said to Arch, and stood waiting, his back to the others. "Someone's got to ride over to White Mountain tonight," he said, reaching for the glass Arch put in front of him. "If it's the Indians someone's got to alert the soldiers over there."

Myer sought a chair and sat down rubbing his eyes as

though he had smoke in them. "Twelve years I been in Grasshopper," he muttered, "and never anything like this before. Twelve years . . ."

Pat Culinan came out of his reverie with a brisk nod and an oath. "I'll ride over," he announced. When Arch held up a bottle and raised his eyebrows, Pat shook his head. "Maybe when I come back," he exclaimed.

Pat would have departed right then but Anvil Wilson appeared outside already astride. As the others crowded to the doorway Anvil said he was going to White Mountain. The others simply stared out at him, all their preconceived notions making them silent and confused about this. They had Anvil pegged as a killer, an outlaw of some kind; anything but a man likely to co-operate with the law.

They didn't say anything. There wasn't much for them to say anyway. Some event was on the verge of overtaking them. They could feel that, could sense its inevitability, so what became gradually uppermost in their minds was simply how and to what extent it was going to affect them.

After Anvil Wilson turned and rode off southward down through town, Arch Pennington stepped back inside and looked at the dead man. "We got to put him some place where he'll stay cool, boys. In this kind of weather it doesn't pay to keep 'em above ground too long. Maybe the army'll send over an ambulance wagon tomorrow. They sure better. Give me a hand; we'll put him in my storeroom for tonight."

They all bent to lift the sergeant, who in life had been a burly, heavy man. After they staggered on through into the storeroom with him, they returned sombrely to Arch's bar and he set up the drinks, on the house. They drank, and afterwards dispersed, for even drinking didn't help allay the uneasiness now.

Chapter Six

PAT CULINAN'S habit of wearing moccasins undoubtedly saved his life that night. Also, the fact that he'd been badly shaken and completely sobered by the sight of that cavalryman dying practically in front of his eyes.

Pat kept an old mangy cat. The critter was spoiled and ungrateful and resentful, but it was Pat's custom to put the varmint outside every night and let it back in every morning.

When Pat left Arch's saloon that night, went to his own place, scooped up his cat and padded silently on out the back way to deposit the cat upon the ground, he didn't make a sound.

There were two men out back. Neither of them heard Pat. Neither of them even saw him, until he straightened up after putting the cat down. He saw them at the same time they saw him. If those two men out there sneaking into town under cover of night could have been forewarned they undoubtedly would have killed Pat with their first shots, but as it turned out they were too startled at Pat's noiselessly silent appearance to shoot straight.

The first bullet struck three feet to Pat's left. The next one hit the log wall of Pat's café overhead. Both those explosions sounded thunderous-loud in the otherwise hushed and brooding darkness. The third bullet hit Pat's back door after he'd let off a squawk, scrambled back inside and slammed it hard. It didn't pass through because the door was made of iron-hard ancient oak, but all the same Pat dropped the bar down locking it, and kept well to one side while he did that.

Everyone in town heard those gunshots. Arch was sitting on the edge of his bed kicking off his boots. Myer was having a snack of rye bread and sausage. Jeff Stone was cleaning his sixgun at his lean-to beside the shop. He was the only one, besides, Pat, who had a gun in his hand when he stepped gingerly out into the night to look and listen. (Pat's cat left Grasshopper and didn't return for fourteen days.)

Pat, in his younger, ruddier days, had been a holy terror at combat. He still had that gorilla-like build, running mostly to flab now, but the power had not all turned soft. He could break a man's neck with his hands and arms and shoulders, drunk or sober, and he was far from being a coward.

The more he moved around, after sneaking out the front of his café, sixgun in hand, the more indignant he became. It was unbelievable that anyone would deliberately attempt to shoot him down for just putting out his cat. He got to the rear corner of his café and strained to catch sounds. There was none to be heard. He dropped low, cocked his sixgun and jumped out crouched and ready. Nothing happened, but behind him Jeff's voice said in quiet disgust, "Get the hell out of in front of me, Pat."

Pat looked back. Jeff came forth from between two buildings lowering his gun as he walked on up to look around. "What did you fire at?" he asked.

Pat screwed up his face. "Me? I didn't fire at nothing. I come out back to put my cat out, and there were two fellers back here. They both fired at me. Come over here by the door an' I'll show you."

They were examining those fresh slashes in the rear of Pat's building when Arch came around back with a shotgun in his hands and a .45 stuffed into his waistband. Arch also looked at the bullet holes. While they were doing this, and puzzling over the unreasonableness of that savage sudden attack, they heard a horse walking down into town from the north. It was so quiet now they could have heard a feather drop.

Arch stood perfectly still, listening. Jeff moved off to scout around over where Pat's attackers had fired from. When he walked back shaking his head, frowning, Pat led the way around front.

They were very careful. One horseman probably couldn't harm them, especially now that they were armed and aroused. Still; caution being the better part of valour, they slipped up where shadows lay thickest and waited. The oncoming horse paced along at a slow but steady gait. Over across the road Myer was standing in his recessed storefront-doorway with a Harper's Ferry army rifle with a barrel long enough and heavy enough to shoot a mile then throw stones. Pat saw Myer over there. So did Arch and Jeff Stone. As that horse came down through the nighttime gloom Myer's big-bored rifle rose higher and higher until it was aimed squarely up where the rider was becoming discernible. Then it suddenly dropped.

The others also lost their hard belligerence. There was a dead soldier tied belly-down across the saddle of that slow-pacing horse. Arch swore under his breath and stepped out to bar the animal's southward progress. The others hung back to give Arch cover until everyone was satisfied no one was skulking around to shoot at Arch, then they congregated out in their moonlighted, dusty roadway.

Jeff Stone bent to look into the dead cavalryman's

face. He afterwards straightened up with a loose head-wag, stuck the pistol into his trousers and reached for the horse's reins. "I'll tell you what I think," he said. "Hour or two after Wilson rides out, here comes another dead soldier."

The others, not yet that organised in their thinking, looked startled. Myer, leaning upon his big-bored Harper's Ferry musket, gazed at Jeff in an expressionless way. "Why?" he asked. No one answered him but Arch Pennington moved in to make a closer inspection of the cavalryman, then stepped back shaking his head. "No sir," he growled. "It couldn't be, Jeff. This man's stiffer'n a ramrod. He was killed some time this afternoon. They don't set up that fast; not in the summertime."

Pat's first comment was more to the point. "Let's get out of the roadway. I don't feel right with my back to the direction them fellers shot at me."

They led the horse around behind Arch's place, carted the corpse into Arch's storeroom, deposited it beside the other cavalryman in there, then went back out to care for the horse. While they were doing that behind the saloon Myer suddenly lifted an arm.

"Listen," he said. "Horses."

They froze, craning around to the left, which was northward. But this time the horses were coming from the south and they were coming fast.

"These are live ones," Arch stated, hefted his shotgun and started over towards the corner of the building. "Maybe Wilson got turned back or something. Maybe he come on to some help before reachin' White Mountain."

The others followed Arch, got almost to the front roadway, when three racing horsemen swept into Grasshopper from the south, guns blazing. Pat dropped flat and yelled for the others to do the same. It was difficult to make out the riders because the blinding flash of their guns drove Myer and Arch and Jeff flat down in the dirt beside Pat. Glass tinkled in the saddleshop window, which didn't matter much; the harness maker had moved on years before, when the army had withdrawn most of its troopers after the last Apache uprising. Bullets struck Myer's store, Jeff's blacksmith shop, and they knocked the louvres out of Arch's batwing, saloon doors.

Arch raised his shotgun and let fly with one barrel. The detonation was thunderous. Arch's scattergun belched a huge gust of orange flame, but the range was too great. If he'd waited five more seconds he could have cut at least one of those raiders down, but as it was he missed, and that sheet of shotgun-flame let the wild-riding horsemen know where at least one defender was. They stopped their erratic firing and turned three sixguns towards the edge of Arch's saloon.

Dust spewed, small clods showered down upon the four prone defenders, lead hit the log walls making the saloon shudder, then the speeding riders were past, half way along towards the north end of town before any of the prone men dared even raise their heads.

Myer got up unsteadily on to one knee and fired his musket. It had a backlash report like a howitzer. The ball was as large as a man's thumb, almost, but Harper's Ferry rifles were notoriously inaccurate at long range, so all that happened was that the bullet tore a fist-sized hole in the door of Pat Culinan's café. Still, it showed defiance, and right then that made the dusty defenders feel much better.

Jeff got off three hand-gun shots, but they too went wild. Jeff was spitting dust and batting his eyes when he fired. He was mad all the way through. Pat never fired at all. He'd been hit flush between the eyes with a pebble the size of an apricot pip and lay there blinking and sucking air.

It was over almost as quickly as it had begun. Up the northward trace they could hear the diminishing rattle of racing horsemen running on down the night.

Pat sat up, felt his forehead and quietly swore. "Dang bullet ploughed up a rock out of the road and hit me right plumb between the horns," he complained. "Dammit all; I need a drink."

Arch agreed with that, arising to beat dust off himself. He stepped out and looked both ways up and down the roadway. His broken louvred door was less than fifteen feet southward. "Come on," he said to the others, and hastened along.

They got inside the *Trails End*. When Pat, still a little groggy, groped for a lamp, Arch growled at him to leave the place dark, went behind his bar and set up four glasses, put his shotgun atop the bar and poured.

"What about that dead soldier?" asked Myer, shuffling over to the bar.

"The hell with him," Arch muttered, pausing long enough to toss off his whisky and to refill his glass. "He's not going anywhere in my storeroom. What about *us*?"

Jeff stood a moment reloading his sixgun and darkly scowling. "That was those three hunters I'll bet you anything," he told the others. "But what in the hell is this all about?"

No one answered; no one even had an opinion to offer. They drank, settling their nerves, and looked at each other in the gloomy barroom. Pat was getting a fine purple lump where that stone had struck him, but it didn't seem to bother him at all. He had his second straight shot and even smiled.

"I reckon they won't try *that* again," he chirped. "Say Myer; did you have that gun double-shotted? Groggy as I was it sounded like the crack of Doom."

Myer merely shrugged without answering. He was far from sharing Pat's quick recovery and good spirits. "Wilson better get back with Marshal Whitsett," he muttered, "or the army—or someone."

"Why?" Pat demanded, reaching for the bottle to pour his third drink. "There are four of us an' only three of them."

Jeff finished reloading, pushed the .45 into his waistband and looked disapprovingly at Pat. "You're crazy," he growled. "There are *five* of 'em. The pair that tried to get you, and the three who went busting through town. Don't tell me those first two were part of the last three, either, because I won't believe you—unless, when daylight comes, we can find where a third one was right at the edge of town holding their horses."

This offered an unsettling question for them to ponder. As Pat reached out for his fourth refill, Arch Pennington reached first, removed the bottle from Pat's locale and leaned over the bar holding it in his fist as he stared towards the door. "Do you suppose," he mused, "there could be more than one bunch of them?"

No one answered him. Pat was beginning to sulk and the others were beginning to get morose and perplexed. "One more drink all around," suggested Pat, eyeing Arch's bottle.

Arch turned, corked the bottle and put it firmly upon his backbar shelf. As he faced back he glared at Pat. "What good'll you be to yourself or the rest of us drunk; you never could handle more'n three at a time and you know it. Now start actin' your age."

That ended that.

Jeff was deep in thought. So was Myer. Between the

pair of them, because they were so different in character, when they spoke again, they offered totally different ideas.

Myer said, "It's not the attack so much as it's *why* we're being attacked. Look at Grasshopper: What is it but a ghost town. There hasn't been anything much here since the army pulled out. Even the harness maker left." Myer waved his arms. "There's enough left for those of us who stay, but what else? I mean; what should anyone want so badly they got to try an' kill Pat, then attack the town for?"

Jeff's dark frown lingered as he said, "That's not the point, Myer. At least not directly. Sure; I wondered about that too, but the point is—will they come back?" Jeff gazed around at his companions. "We're not the army; we're not soldiers. We don't even have a defence plan, an' if we did have, what good would it do against men who skulk into town in the night? What we got to do is organise some kind of defence. We got to have sentries out and all that kind of stuff, because whoever those fellers are, they're not here for the hunting, you can bet your last dollar on that. Before this mess is over with, someone's goin' to get killed. You can bet on that too."

Arch waited until Jeff finished, then said, "Jeff; something you can do right off to set things straight. You can tell us what you know about Anvil Wilson, because unless I'm a mile off, Anvil Wilson's in this thing up to the armpits."

Jeff glanced briefly at Arch, then dropped his eyes. He was a doggedly stubborn man, but also, in calm moments, he wasn't entirely unreasonable. But when he had to make this kind of a decision, he did it slowly, so, while the others watched him and waited, he came to his slow decision.

"Manhunter," he eventually mumbled.

"Manhunter?" Arch said. "You mean a bounty hunter?"

"I don't know," replied Jeff. "All I know for a fact is what I was told down south. They called him The Man From Cody County. They said he tracked down other men. They said he was as bad with a gun as any man living, but no one ever told me whether he was a bounty hunter, a lawman, or just one of those gunfighters who go aroun' lookin' for trouble. They *did* say he was a good one to stay well clear of, though, so, when he showed up here, I kept out of his way and kept what I knew of him to myself."

Jeff reached for his glass, downed his last drink, and said no more.

Chapter Seven

PAT'S cat didn't return and furthermore, when daylight arrived and he saw where Myer's musket ball had smashed his door he got indignant all over again.

Arch and Jeff climbed to the roof of Myer's store, the highest building in Grasshopper, and, using a spyglass Myer provided, made a very minute study of the surrounding countryside. They were still up there when two horsemen appeared, not too long after daybreak, riding in a slow lope from the easterly direction of White Mountain. Jeff closed the spyglass and said, "Carl Whitsett and Anvil Wilson. We better get down and let the others know."

Arch did not at once respond. He was lying upon his stomach gazing off towards the sunlighted west where those three horsemen had appeared upon a middle-distance ridge. "They're still around," he muttered, squinting ahead. "They weren't Flying R cowhands raising a little hell, and they sure weren't Injuns, so they're still somewhere around, Jeff."

Stone didn't dispute that but he arose and started over to the crawl-hole leading down inside Myer's store. Arch eventually followed him.

None of them had retired after the attack, they had sat around Arch's saloon waiting for daylight. They had then gone all around the outskirts of town looking for the place where someone might have stood, holding three horses, while those first two men had crept up and shot at Pat Culinan.

What they'd actually found had added to their growing mystery. The two skulkers had come alone, had
tied their horses not a hundred yards from where they'd
shot at Pat, and after that event, had fled back to their
animals, got astride, spun around and fled westerly.
Also, they back-tracked those other three raiders who
had charged through Grasshopper firing, and discovered
that these men hadn't been skulking around town, but
had come up the southward trace riding hard.

What all this meant, as Jeff pointed out, was that
his guess of the night before, had probably been correct : There were *two* bunches of strangers setting themselves against the town, not one bunch.

When Anvil Wilson and Carl Whitsett arrived, Myer
and Pat, along with Jeff and Arch Pennington, were
waiting for them over in front of Culinan's café. They
recounted all that had happened and escorted Wilson
and Whitsett over to Arch's storeroom to view the dead
cavalrymen. After that, Marshal Whitsett bought a
round of drinks and asked a lot of questions, while
Anvil Wilson strolled out of the saloon and made a
complete circuit of town before coming back to report
that the evidence of a rough fight bore out everything
he and Whitsett had been told.

That stung Arch, who looked frostily at Wilson and
said, "Mister; if you figured we made all this up, just
stick around Grasshopper for when they come back
again."

Marshal Whitsett calmed Arch by stating that he
meant to do just exactly that—stay in Grasshopper for
a few days.

Myer wasn't too impressed. He said, "Where's the
army? They got two dead men here. They should send
over a company, maybe, and a cannon or something."

Whitsett's reply to that turned them all silent. "The

army's gone after a band of Mex raiders who hit a ranch west of White Mountain, running off a big band of prized horses. I sent word to the captain what has happened over here, but at the best he can't even receive my message for three or four days."

Anvil Wilson went to the bar and planted a coin down calling for ale. Arch served him, but like the others, Arch was listening to Marshal Whitsett. When the lawman finished Arch said, "What about that squad these dead ones belonged to, Marshal? It's still up in the mountains somewhere. And one more thing—what was them soldiers doin' around here anyway? They didn't even come into town, but made their camp back beside the creek. I sold the sergeant one bottle of whisky. He wouldn't tell me a thing."

Anvil Wilson was holding his glass of ale when he said, "Start at the beginning," to Carl Whitsett. "They're in it up to their ears now. They're right about those men coming back, too, so it seems to me they've got a right to know."

Whitsett deliberated. He was at least in this respect, a little like Jeff Stone. He made no hasty decisions and spoke just when he had something to say.

"Know what?" Pat asked, looking around. "What the devil's goin' on?"

Wilson set aside his ale, fished in a pocket and brought forth an odd little badge which he put atop the bar. He and Carl Whitsett were looking at one another. Whitsett still said nothing.

"I'm an agent for the office of the Adjutant General," said Wilson. "That's sort of like being a U.S. Marshal, except that I'm an army officer who deals almost exclusively with army problems."

Arch, studying the little badge closely, said, "A civilian; you mean you're a civilian army officer?"

"Something like that," replied Wilson. "I hold a major's commission in the Regular Army, but my job is kind of a cross between a U.S. Marshal and a secret service operative. Whatever concerns the army, concerns me. But where troopers in uniform have a limited variety of authority, I have the authority to act in either capacity—as a soldier or as a civilian lawman." Wilson nodded towards Marshal Whitsett. "If I'm not making myself very clear about this, ask the marshal there; he can tell you what a man from the Adjutant General's office is, and what such a man has authority to do."

Whitsett nodded as the townsmen glanced over at him. "It's like Major Wilson says. He has more authority than a soldier in uniform, or than I have as a deputy U.S. marshal. I can't interfere with uniformed soldiers but he can, being one himself."

Jeff Stone's puzzlement prompted him to say, "*Major* Wilson. When I saw you down around the border, they told me you were a manhunter of some kind. No one seemed to know just what you were, exactly, but they sure didn't have you figured for any army officer."

"I track down deserters," Anvil told Jeff and the others. "I also try to intercept contraband army weapons and supplies being sold over the border by U.S. troopers. I go after anyone, civilian or soldier, who is working against either the armed forces of the country, or directly against the country itself, such as Mex guerillas." Anvil smiled that quick, ready smile of his. "If that's bein' a manhunter, why then I reckon that's what I am."

Jeff's face slowly cleared. He breathed an audible sigh. "That takes a load off my mind," he stated. "I had you pegged as something altogether different."

Myer Frankel wasn't particularly impressed; he was instead concerned with the present dilemma of Grasshopper. "Major," he exclaimed. "This thing you wanted the marshal to explain to us—what is it? What's worrying us here in Grasshopper is what's going on. Why should a storekeeper, a saloonman, a blacksmith and a café keeper be attacked by two bands of outlaws in a town that's sliding slowly into oblivion? What have we got; what have we done?"

Carl Whitsett had eventually come to his decision, so he said, "Myer; it's not you fellers, particularly, and it's sure not the town of Grasshopper. A month ago a band of outlaws robbed the paymaster on his way between Fort Apache and the outlying army posts. He was carrying the pay and supply money, something close to eighteen thousand dollars, which kept the outposts like White Mountain, operating."

"All right," stated Myer. "But why us? We got no soldiers stationed at Grasshopper. We got no . . ."

"Let him finish," said Anvil Wilson. "Go ahead, Carl."

Marshal Whitsett continued speaking. "The robbery took place south and east of White Mountain. That means, the outlaws came down out of the mountains, and we know for a fact they went back up into them again. We didn't find the paymaster or his escort for three days. That gave the outlaws a big lead."

"Wait a second," broke in Arch Pennington. "This paymaster an' his escort—dead, Marshal?"

Whitsett nodded. "Shot to pieces, Arch. Killed the same way those two men in your back room were killed."

Arch slumped across his bar. Jeff and Pat, also leaning along the bar, exchanged a look with Arch. All three of them turned silent and solemn as Carl Whitsett finished what he had to say.

"Something happened, though, after that robbery. We found a dead outlaw—shot in the back—where some men'd had a hidden camp in the mountains. That's when the army sent for Anvil Wilson. I didn't know he was coming; didn't even know anything about him, until after he hit Grasshopper."

Wilson took it from there, saying, "When I came here I wasn't sure but what one of you fellers could be involved. That's why I let you sweat. It's also why I rode out now and then snooping around. I lay up on the slopes waiting for someone from Grasshopper to ride out fast and head for the outlaw hideout back in the mountains. None of you ever did, so I cultivated old John West, and got a thorough run-down on each of you."

"Wait a second," Arch Pennington said, breaking in again. "Are you tellin' us the outlaws who killed the paymaster and stole his eighteen thousand dollars are still in the White Mountains?"

"I'll tell you something even better," replied Anvil. "I'll tell you that the reason they're still in the mountains is because one member of the original outlaw gang got word to another band of renegades where the thieves hid that money, and now there are *two* bands skulking through the mountains, one trying to get out with the money, the other band trying to prevent that, at the same time they're trying to also get that cash."

Jeff turned and thumped the bar with his balled fist. "A drink, Arch," he growled. "I need some bolstering. Bad enough hearing I've been plumb wrong about Major Wilson, but being right last night when I figured there had to be two gangs against us, is still worse."

Arch set up the bottle. Pat moved silently over beside Jeff and hopefully motioned for a glass too. Arch was so preoccupied with his thoughts he forgot and gave Pat a shot.

"But why the town?" Myer inquired of Anvil Wilson. "There are no outlaws here."

Before Wilson could answer Pat Culinan choked, set

aside his glass, batted excess water from his eyes and said, "Damn! Those three hunters!"

Wilson smiled at Pat. "Give him another slug of the stuff," he told Arch. "He just earned it. Those hunters are what's left of the original five men who held up the paymaster. I found one of their crew shot in the back at their secret camp. The other one's with that second bunch who are trying to get the money too."

Marshal Whitsett, seeing the grave expressions around him, said, "We figure the reason they attacked Grasshopper last night might have been to smoke out anyone here who could be working with one gang or the other one."

"Or," said Anvil Wilson, "because, when those hunters were here, they hid the cash somewhere around Grasshopper. If they did that they'd come back for it. Also, if the other bunch suspected that's what happened, they'd raid Grasshopper too. You understand, boys?"

"You ought to see the front door of my café if you don't think we understand," exclaimed Pat. He got another of those sudden flashes and said, speaking sharply, "Hey; where did those hunters stay when they lay over for a day around here? If they hid that eighteen thousand, it'll be likely be somewhere near that place, won't it?"

Jeff and Arch exchanged a look, both reflecting on what Pat was suggesting. Jeff dryly said, "Maybe, in their boots, and for that kind of money, I'd have shot up the town too."

But none of them knew where the hunters had stayed, except that they'd hung out in Arch's saloon. There was a vague notion among them that the outlaws had camped somewhere north of town, but Anvil Wilson, who had been absent from Grasshopper the day the outlaws had come into town, didn't believe that; he sug-

gested the renegades must have at least by that time
suspected they were being shadowed by the second gang.

"If they hid it anywhere," he proposed, "it's right
here in Grasshopper." When the others questioned
that, Anvil had a sound enough reason to advance for his
idea. "They knew someone was watching them. They
had to know that by the time they came down here to
Grasshopper, because by then one of their crew had
joined up with his other friends, and also because someone had back-shot another of their gang. They wouldn't
hide that cash at some outlying camp for the simple
reason that they'd know, as soon as they pulled out, the
watchers would have all the time they needed to dig
up their cache. On the other hand, boys, they'd also
know that, with you fellers always around town here, the
second bunch couldn't just ride in and start taking your
town apart. That's why I believe they hid it right here.
That's also why I think both gangs were here last night.
One bunch to retrieve their money, the other bunch to
try and find it before it was retrieved."

Myer Frankel threw up his hands and rolled up his
eyes. "I run a store," he wailed. "I mind my own
business, don't buy trinkets from the Indians, make a living and drink a little whisky in the evening. Now look
at me; up to my ears in a mess over something that I got
no interest in, but which could get me killed. I ask you:
What's happening to Grasshopper?"

"Nothing—yet," said Marshal Whitsett, and strolled
across to gaze up and down the empty roadway with his
lips pursed and his eyes narrowed. "There's a lot of
country out there, Major," he said to Anvil Wilson.
"I reckon what you figured on the ride over here is
right. Instead of making possemen out of these fellers
and trying to run those gangs down, we'd do better to
just sit back here and let them bring their war to us."

"War," croaked Myer. "My gawd; just what I need in my late years, a war." He got up and walked out of the saloon, down to his store and disappeared inside, down there.

Chapter Eight

MARSHAL WHITSETT and Anvil Wilson ate their
noon-day meal over at Pat's café. Culinan had an endless score of theories to advance before the law officers
got out of his establishment, took their horses and left
Grasshopper riding northward.

Arch and Myer and Jeff Stone watched them go,
feeling lonely, or, as Arch said, "You got to be crazy to
ride up into those mountains like that, with two bunches
of outlaws spyin' on you every inch o' the way and
perhaps waitin' to massacre you."

Jeff had a different feeling about that. "Of all the
folks I wouldn't want to try an' massacre, those two top
the list."

Still; they agreed they'd have felt a lot better if the
lawmen had remained in town that afternoon, and
when Pat came over with his news they wished it all
the harder.

"Hey," Pat called out as he padded across the road.
"Which one of you took my horse?"

They looked around at Pat. Myer said, "What're
you talking about? Who'd want your horse?"

"Well someone did because they took him out'n the
public corral."

Arch groaned aloud, stepped off the plankwalk and
started walking. The others followed. They trooped up to
the log corral, lined up like a set of crows along its
roadside bars and looked in. "Mine too," said Arch.
"An' your horse as well, Jeff." Myer flapped his arms.

"That settles it," he said. "They're all around us. They got us bottled up in Grasshopper like a bunch of flies in a spider's web. No horses; what's next—our guns?" He looked at the others. "An' I'll make you a bet—those lawmen won't get back either."

Jeff stuck to his earlier assessments concerning that likelihood, saying, "They'll get back. No one's goin' to drygulch that pair."

"Sure," muttered Myer. "Sure they'll come back— like that red-faced sergeant and his trooper came back."

Arch hung upon the corral stringers studying the yonder run of wild country. He eventually turned to Jeff and said, "You were right, Jeff, we got to organise ourselves into a defence unit with sentries and such-like. Let's go over to my place and have a cool beer an' talk about that."

They never got there.

Pat Culinan turned first, eager to have his cool beer, but he stopped dead-still in his tracks. In a very soft, low tone Pat said, "Look southward, fellers, an' don't do anythin' foolish."

They all turned to look. Entering town from the southern trail were Pert Fox, Cap Beeson and Wes Hall, the hunters who had turned out not to be hunters; at least not pot-hunters. They were riding slowly and carefully, watching every window and doorway and rooftop as they came steadily up towards the centre of town.

"You armed?" Pat asked his friends. They weren't; not even Arch, who usually wore his sixgun. "Well," said Pat, "don't feel bad, neither am I. But if this comes off 'thout anyone gettin' hurt, from now on I aim to be—night and day."

They didn't say any more. Fox and his outlaw friends were getting close. No one, in fact, spoke at all, until the outlaws halted about fifteen feet off and stared down from their saddles at the townsmen. Fox flicked a look over at the corral, on around at the other buildings, then he said, "What's the matter, boys, you look like you just lost your last friend."

"Lost our horses," Arch grumbled. "They were right here in this corral. Now they're gone."

Pert's black eyes ironically shone. "Too bad," he said. "But if you can't leave Grasshopper, you can't bring in no outsiders, can you?"

Jeff shook his head exasperatedly, "What outsiders? No one ever comes here."

"The law came here," contradicted Pert Fox. "We saw that deputy marshal from White Mountain ride in this morning. We also saw him ride out with another feller."

"He's got that right," retorted Arch Pennington.

Fox looked them over then gently inclined his head. "Sure he has. He's the law. The law can go anywhere. Who was that feller he rode out with?"

"Just a drifter," stated Pat Culinan. "A feller who came around a week or two back."

Fox looked straight at Arch. "You told me no strangers came to Grasshopper, saloonman. How about that feller?"

"Didn't figure him as a stranger after he'd been loafin' around here for a week, Mister Fox. Sometimes those drifters pass through. No one pays much attention to them."

Pert Fox was satisfied with that. He said, "Yeah; now tell me he come here all alone."

"He did," Arch replied. "Rode in alone about a week back. No one's met him here an' as far as we know he didn't go out an' meet no one."

Jeff Stone regarded the three outlaws without fear, his expression antagonistic. "Was it you fellers busted through here last night shootin' up the town?" he asked.

The outlaw called Wes Hall leaned in his saddle and gave Jeff look for look. "What if it was?" he asked. "You goin' to take us over your knee, blacksmith?"

The others knew Jeff well enough to know he'd fight at the drop of a hat—or a challenge. They began talking, began striving hard to avert serious trouble right there. It was Myer who finally made the telling remark when he said to Pert Fox: "Listen; whatever it is around here you want—take it and go away. We're not troublesome men. We live here and trade here. Beyond that we got no interest in trouble."

Pert turned and snarled at Hall to shut up. Wes did, but he and Jeff had by that time hardened into strong personal enemies. Pert said, "That's why we're here, boys. We left something in your town the other day. Now we're back to get it and ride on."

"So get it," Myer told Fox, and made a wide gesture with his hands. "If it's something we got nothing to do with—get it in good health, and then ride on."

Pert's long upper lip drew back disclosing big white teeth. He leaned forward, braced against the saddle-horn and swung down. He was still expansively smiling when he said, "That's what we like, boys, co-operation. Wes; you come with me. Cap; watch these fellers. They won't make no trouble but watch 'em all the same."

Pert Fox and Wes Hall walked anglingly up towards Arch's bar. The townsmen watched them, each in his secret heart wondering if that's where they had cached their stolen money. Arch looked the most dumbfounded of them all. When his curiosity was at its height he turned towards Cap Beeson and asked one question.

"They had it cached in my saloon?"

Beeson, a stringy individual, younger than either of his companions, turned his bitter and dissipated face towards Arch and raised both eyebrows. "Cached what?" he asked.

Arch faintly reddened. "Well," he muttered, "whatever it is they're after."

Beeson kept eyeing Arch without replying, his expression turning suspicious and sceptical. After a long moment he said, "Which one of you idiots had a shotgun last night when we come through?"

None of the townsmen answered. Beeson dropped his right hand until it rested upon his holstered sixgun. In that threatening stance he waited a little longer. Still, no one answered him.

Beeson kept his hand upon his pistol, but he shrugged disdainfully. "Never mind. It don't matter now." Across the road Fox and Hall were coming out of the *Trails End*, each lugging a heavy canvas sack reinforced at top and bottom with dark strips of thick leather.

Arch swallowed with a visible effort. He'd had eighteen thousand dollars in cold coin in his saloon and hadn't even known it. How those outlaws had managed to hide it there, and just exactly where they'd hidden it, almost made Arch ask another question, but in the end he didn't because something happened to divert them all.

A gunshot rang out from the same side of the road they were standing upon, somewhere over behind Pat Culinan's café. Wes Hall, in the act of stepping off the plankwalk over there, missed his step and went down in the powdery dust, losing his canvas bag. At once Pert Fox sprang back under Arch's wooden overhang and drew his gun. At the same time Cap Beeson ripped out a wild curse, jumped in closer to the corral and fired twice in the direction of that solitary gunshot.

Jeff and Myer dropped flat. Pat Culinan and Arch

Pennington followed their prudent example. Fox bawled some kind of an order at Beeson. He began edging along the corral northward. Fox bawled out another order and Beeson changed his course, heading over where their horses stood.

Two more shots came from over behind the westward buildings. Wes Hall was struggling to arise. One of those bullets flung roadway dirt in his face. He raised both hands to dig at his eyes. He was fiercely swearing.

Beeson got their horses, kept an animal on each side of him, and began turning to head over closer, protected like that, where the invisible attackers were hiding among the buildings. Pert Fox, whatever else he was, was no coward. He ran out to Wes Hall, yanked him upright and gave him a push. Those two advanced straight across the road, Hall clawing at his holstered sixgun and blinking furiously to clear the tears from his eyes.

Fox's strategy was elemental. He meant to hunt down those hidden men by using the horses as shields. It might have worked too, because it was a bold scheme, and also because Pert Fox was an expert pistolman, except that the hidden attackers suddenly changed their tactics, ran swiftly northward and when they began firing again, were almost directly across from Arch's saloon. Their strategy was also transparent; both those canvas bags full of money lay over in front of the *Trails End*; whether the hiding men meant to kill Fox and his friends or not, was never determined, because right then they were much more interested in the gold.

But Fox and Beeson recognised their peril instantly and turned northward again, rushing over to get flat up against Pat's building. Wes Hall was still half blinded, but at last he opened with his sixgun too. He limped past where the four prone men were lying and Jeff saw blood on his lower leg where a bullet had creased him.

Pat would have jumped up and run into his café when the three outlaws moved past northward, concentrating upon their enemies, but Arch caught him by the shoulder and heaved all his weight against Culinan.

"Stay down, you fool," Arch hissed. "It's not our fight. Let 'em kill one another."

Pat subsided.

It seemed that there were three men on each side. Fox and Hall and Beeson against the invisible three attackers. It seemed that way right up until Fox and his friends were parallel with the front of the saloon, across the road, making their shots tell against the hidden men. But at the most crucial point in this fierce little brief fight, two more guns opened up from down by the jailhouse. Lead slashed into log walls behind Fox, Beeson, and Wes Hall, bringing them suddenly back around to face this fresh attack.

"Five of 'em," growled Jeff Stone, raising his head just enough to see southward. "They'll get Fox and his pardners now. They got 'em between two fires."

It perhaps might have worked out that way, but Fox didn't frighten easily. He stepped into a recessed doorway to reload while Beeson and Hall blazed away in both directions, holding their enemies in check. When Fox was ready again, he stepped forth and raised his sixgun. None of the rigidly braced men on the ground back by Pat's café could see what he was doing, but when Fox fired, a man over across the roadway southward of Myer's store, plunged forward from between two abandoned buildings, threw up his hands and flopped out into the roadway.

That was the turning point. Fox said something harsh to Beeson and Hall. The three of them turned and raced back where their horses were, sprang astride, spun the animals and spurred savagely southward. One man down there got off a single shot as they thundered past, but the three of them drove him back under cover with a volley of murderous gunfire.

As suddenly as it began, the fight was over. Out behind town Jeff and Pat, Myer and Arch, heard other horsemen suddenly break away in a wild race southward, too. The four of them sat up gingerly, looking up where those two canvas bags still lay in the dusty roadway out front of Arch's saloon.

Chapter Nine

"WHAT in the almighty hell," muttered Arch, beating dust off himself. "They didn't any of them take the gold."

Jeff Stone was the last one to arise. He kept looking southward. Somewhere down there, far off, several guns faintly boomed as the deadly chase went on. Jeff turned and also looked up where the money bags were lying in hot morning sunlight. He started walking.

They took the bags into Arch's place, heaved them atop the bar, and while Arch poured them all a backbone stiffener, they eyed the things.

"Eighteen thousand in gold coin," said Pat Culinan, his voice full of solemn awe. "Lord; that's more'n a man could make in half a lifetime."

"In a *whole* lifetime," stated Arch, holding a full shot glass in his big fist. "They had it hid in here all the time."

Myer, also holding his shot glass and making no move to down the liquor, said, "They'll be back. They got some private feud going between 'em, but don't you ever think they won't be back. Their kind'd burn this town to the ground and massacre every one of us for that gold." Myer gazed disconsolately at the canvas sacks a moment, then firmly placed his untouched drink atop the bar and started walking.

"Hey," Arch called. "Where you going?"

"To get my rifle," replied Myer, over near the door. "And I'd advise you fellers to get your guns too."

"Wait a minute, consarn it," protested Arch as the others also began heading for the door. "What about these sacks? We can't just leave 'em lyin' here atop my bar."

"I can," stated Myer, reaching up to push through the broken batwing doors. "That money's going to get men killed. I like money as well as the next man. But not *that* well. You ever hear of a dead man spending money, Arch?"

"Dead man hell," stormed Pennington. "You come back here and help me get rid of this stuff. I don't want it in my saloon if those fellers come back."

Jeff and Pat started back to the bar but not Myer. He walked on out into the gunpowder-scented bright-hot morning heading straight down to his store.

"Danged monkey," Arch growled. "He's in this as much as the rest of us."

Jeff shrugged Arch's annoyance off. "He'll be back, Arch. But that's not what we've got to sweat over right now. What'll we do with these sacks?"

"Give 'em to Marshal Whitsett and Major Wilson," exclaimed Pat. "That's what they're here for. At least, that's what they *were* here for. Maybe now they'll never come back." Pat sidled over where Myer's untouched shot glass was, lifted it and dropped the liquid lightning straight down. His eyes sprang water and his face contorted, but he didn't make a sound.

"Well I don't want this danged stuff in my saloon," Arch stated, with a black scowl. "I don't want any part of that kind of money. Jeff . . ."

"No you don't," snapped the blacksmith. "You don't get me to take it over to my place."

"Then where, damn it?" Arch demanded.

"It won't matter where we take it," Pat put in. "Those outlaws will be back for it. Except for those two lawmen I'd say take it out to the edge of town an' hang it from a tree limb. Let anyone who wants it come get it. Otherwise we're goin' to get hit by those cussed gunmen again."

The roadway doors opened and Myer strolled back in carrying his big-bored old Harper's Ferry musket. He was perspiring because it was now well along towards midday and the heat was piling up outside again, giving the air a dry, metallic scent and taste.

"Two riders coming from the north," announced Myer from over by the door. "I'm hoping it's Whitsett and Wilson."

It was. But what Myer in his haste had neglected to notice was that there was a third and fourth rider, each riding directly behind the first two horsemen. The others saw this as soon as they went over to crowd around the doorway peering up where blazing sunlight palely brightened those oncoming horsemen.

"Soldiers," said Jeff, stepping through the doors out upon the decaying old plankwalk. "Two of the soldiers from that squad that passed through the other day."

Whitsett and Wilson were in the lead. They entered Grasshopper side by side, the troopers riding the same way four feet farther back. The entire quartet moved slowly and steadily, as though they anticipated no trouble, as though they were lost deep down in their own thoughts, which they were.

When they angled over to tie up in front of Arch's saloon, they gazed at the embattled townsmen, but didn't say a word until they had all dismounted and tied up. Then they didn't speak until Pat said, "Boys; if you value them horses, you better fetch 'em right on up into the saloon with you."

Whitsett put a quizzical glance upon Culinan, but Anvil Wilson turned his head and gazed across at the empty public corral. "What happened?" he asked, turning back.

"We had visitors," Arch said, and moved aside to hold open his broken doors. "Step in here and look what we got on the bar."

Whitsett, Wilson, the two grey-faced, dusty, sweaty, cavalrymen entered, approached the bar and halted when they were close enough to recognise those army paymaster canvas bags.

Anvil looked at the townsmen. "Where did these come from?" he inquired, laying a hand upon one of the bags to test its solid contents.

Arch explained, with an occasional assist from Jeff or Myer or Pat. When he finished Myer said, "Marshal Whitsett; do us all a favour and get that money out of Grasshopper. I'm telling you, those men'll be back. They got some kind of bad blood between them, but that don't mean they're going to forget the sacks are here. They all know the money is here."

Anvil said, "It wouldn't make any difference, Myer, whether we took the money over to White Mountain or not. They'll still come back and hit your town. Besides, we have these two survivors of an ambush up in the mountains with us; they're both hurt and tuckered out." Anvil nodded over where the pair of dull-eyed, rumpled cavalrymen had sank down upon chairs near one of Arch's poker tables. "We couldn't possibly leave Grasshopper with the money until tomorrow morning."

Myer shrugged, accepting this philosophically, but he persisted in his entreaty. "All right, spend the night here. Maybe that'll be best anyway. But please—in the morning take the soldiers and the money and leave Grasshopper."

"If they can," Pat said from the bar. "If they leave their danged horses outside like they're doin' right now

I'll give you big odds they'll be afoot just like we are, come sunup."

One of the troopers got up, walked to the bar, wordlessly dropped a coin and waited for Arch to bring two glasses of ale. He then, still without a word being said, returned to the table and set one of the glasses in front of his companion. Not until both soldiers had been revived by that ale, did either of them shake out of a deep-down thraldom which had evidently held both men in its grip for a considerable length of time.

One of them wasn't more than eighteen or nineteen years of age, fair and clear-eyed, tall and supple. The other one was older, perhaps thirty, with a thin, crescent scar along the curve of his left jaw. It looked like some kind of an edged weapon had made that scar, and the soldier's eyes, sunken now and vaguely glazed, still showed something coiled and venomous in their depths.

It was the older trooper who finally spoke, after downing his ale and signalling Arch for a re-fill. He said, "If you're feelin' sorry for 'em—don't. They never knew what hit 'em. One minute we was ridin' up the trail, one scout out ahead, the next minute they let us have it from both sides. It's a damned miracle me'n the kid here got away. Wouldn't have, I expect, but our horses stampeded. Sergeant Kirk's critter also ran off. But I saw him take a bad one before he passed from sight through the trees. The kid? well—I guess seein' 'em all droppin' like flies on both sides like that, sort of muddled him. They were friends, barracks mates and campground comrades. Maybe that don't mean much to you civilians, but it means a lot to a trooper. Especially a kid like him."

"How did he get out of it?" Anvil Wilson asked.

"I saw him with that glassy look sittin' there with lead flyin' all around, so as I went past I grabbed the reins. About then somethin' stung his cussed horse. He shot past like I was tied to a tree."

Jeff Stone asked who the ambushers were. The soldier simply pulled down his mouth and shook his head. Marshal Whitsett persisted in this too, but all they could get from the trooper was that all he'd been able to see was firing guns on both sides of the trail, his comrades dropping, and nothing to shoot back at. It was, he told them, like a genuine oldtime Apache ambush, except that these had to be white men because they were much better shots.

Something which was uppermost in Arch's mind came out now. "The sergeant had just enough life left in him to walk through those doors yonder, before he cashed in. But how did that other one get tied across his saddle an' his horse set on the right trail smack-dab into Grasshopper?"

Anvil Wilson said softly, "Someone's idea of a joke— or a warning. This Pert Fox you've spoken of; does he look like the kind that would do something like that?"

"Lordy yes," exclaimed Pat Culinan. "He's the type to throw stones at his own grandmaw, poor old lady."

Myer had turned reflective after listening to the soldier's story. Now he said, "Tell me; how many men were in that ambush?"

"I don't know," replied the trooper. "As I said—all hell busted loose in one second."

"I know," Myer persisted, leaning forward in his chair. "But was it a hundred guns, fifty guns, maybe five or ten."

"Five or ten," the trooper replied.

Myer leaned back looking exultant. "All right. This much we now know; it wasn't Pert Fox's outfit, because there are only three of them. It was the other bunch—

until Fox shot one of those men, there were five of them."

"Shot one?" Anvil Wilson said, looking interested.

"Forget it," said Arch. "He's dead. I went down and dragged him into the building where the pool room used to be. There's not a damned thing on him but his gun, a plug of chawin', and six silver dollars—which I appropriated as a contribution towards fixin' my batwing doors." Arch took the fresh refills to the soldiers' table, bent and gazed quizzically, peering into the grey, blank face of the younger trooper, straightened up with a grunt and went back around his bar where he suddenly remembered something and said, "Major; what about these dead men; we can't leave 'em unburied after today. Take it from me, two days above ground in midsummer Arizona, and a block o' granite'll start sourin'."

"Bury them," Wilson answered. "I've got their identification. You can bury them any time you like."

Arch looked at Anvil Wilson like the Adjutant General's man was slow poison. Whether he meant to say anything or not, he didn't get the opportunity. Myer beat him to it. Myer had taken only a minimal part in their discussions. Now he showed how his thoughts had been running when he said, "Listen; does anyone know who those other five—four—men are? I mean, how do you fight phantoms?"

"Phantoms my foot," exclaimed Pat Culinan. "You never seen phantoms shoot like them fellers did. Peppered the danged front of my café."

Anvil Wilson, ignoring Pat, wagged his head at Myer. "The only thing we know is that they are not the ones who originally stole these sacks of money. What we don't exactly know, but what we're reasonably certain of, is, as I've already explained, one of Pert Fox's crew double-crossed Fox and had some cronies of his own waiting when Fox came back into the mountains after robbing the paymaster. Who they are, where they came from, no one's had the time to ascertain yet. But none of that's important right now anyway, Myer. What's important is keeping this money and keeping alive."

"Nice," murmured Myer. "That's all very neat and nice. Maybe you got some notion how we do that?" When neither of the lawmen answered him, Myer looked at his fellow townsmen and said, "I been thinking. Fox figures he isn't goin' to get this money, let's say. Let's also figure for the moment those other outlaws come to the same conclusion. You know what I think? They'll combine forces." Myer looked from face to face.

For a moment they were all silent, then Jeff Stone said, "No; I don't think so, Myer. Didn't you see how that second bunch took out of town after Fox an' Beeson an' Hall? There's no love lost between those two crews."

Myer softly said, "For eighteen thousand dollars, Jeff?" And left it like that, his meaning painfully clear. The opposing gangs of renegades might be enemies, but at the prospect of losing the money, would they remain enemies, or would they bury the hatchet, combine forces and try to get the gold?

"He's got a point," murmured Marshal Whitsett, turning to calmly eye the canvas pouches. "This stuff could get some men killed before it's taken back to White Mountain and turned over to the army."

Pat Culinan padded across to the door, his moccasined feet making no sound at all. He looked out where those four drowsing horses stood at the tie-rack. He also made a careful survey of the yonder buildings over across the roadway on either side of his café.

"Awful quiet," he murmured. "Too danged quiet, if you ask me." He started to turn away, then halted, looking northward. His stance, his total silence, drew the others over where he was looking.

A solitary rider was entering Grasshopper from the west. He had a long-barrelled rifle balanced across his lap. His hatbrim was tugged low to shield eyes that seemed to be rummaging each splash of hot sunlight and each shallow angle of building shade.

"It's not Fox," someone muttered. "He's not heavy enough."

Marshal Whitsett and Anvil Wilson pushed through and walked out upon the old plankwalk where they stopped about ten feet apart, watching.

The stranger wasn't recognisable because of the yellow, blinding sunlight, until he got well into town. It was old John West, riding a handsome chestnut gelding with tiny ears and powerful forearms.

"Something's bothering him," said Anvil Wilson. "He's not carrying that rifle across his lap for the fun of it."

John saw them leaving the saloon to crowd out around the pair of lawmen and reined over towards the saloon. When he was close enough for them to make it out, they saw that his face was settled in an iron-like expression, with the old eyes slitted and restless.

John drew rein, turned, spat, turned back and gazed at the townsmen and the brace of law officers. "Hell of a country this is gettin' to be when a feller can't even raise a few horses 'thout danged thieves robbin' him in the night." He fixed a hostile look upon Carl Whitsett, whom he'd known a number of years. "Where's the danged law when a man needs it, I'd like to know?"

Whitsett said, "Get down, John. Come inside where we can talk."

Old John slewed his wrathy glance over the front of

Arch's saloon, then over Arch himself. "I wouldn't step inside that place if my guts were on fire an' he had the only water," he growled. But he dismounted, tied his horse and moved over into the shade. In response to Anvil Wilson's question, he said, "Lost four head of my best broke horses. I didn't find 'em gone until sun-up, then I went trackin'. It was four fellers on foot snuck in and stoled 'em right out'n my barn. How d'you like that? Right out'n my consarned barn." John rested his rifle butt-down, hooked both skinny arms around it and spat amber out into the roadway dust. "I found their wore-out horses up a draw. Wyoming brands on all of 'em. They'd ridden those horses just about into the ground, too, like maybe they'd been chased—or had been chasin' someone else."

Arch turned and went inside his saloon. He re-emerged moments later with a tall glass of cool ale which he shoved at West. "Drink it," he growled. "You're dry'n hot. Forget that silly argument we had. Drink it down."

Old John looked acidly at Arch. "This your way of apologisin'?" he asked.

Arch reddened, but he nodded. "If you want it that way, John," he said.

John took the glass, threw back his head and downed the ale. Then he smiled flintily at Arch. "Somethin' good come out'n it after all," he said, turned and pushed on inside the saloon.

Everyone but Anvil Wilson and Carl Whitsett trooped back inside behind old John West. Those two stood out there a moment longer to look out where afternoon was settling in.

Chapter Ten

IT WAS near three o'clock when the subject came up again about burying the two dead troopers and that dead outlaw. Arch bucked like a bay steer. "The ground this time o' year's harder'n the hubs of hell. Besides; why us fellers here in town?"

"Who else?" Marshal Whitsett asked. "You want 'em lying around here for a week or so until I fetch over a grave detail when the soldiers come back from their sortie?"

Arch didn't want that, but he only very reluctantly went along with the others, who got tools and hiked down south of town where there was a weed-grown, rank little boot-hill cemetery.

It was a dehydratingly hot afternoon. They worked in shifts. The only one among them still talking was Arch. He had something to say with each shovelful of earth he tossed aside. The pair of troopers didn't go down to the cemetery. No one asked them to. The older man had a bullet-creased side and the younger one was still in shock. Then, when Jeff and Myer, Arch and Pat returned for the bodies along with Marshal Whitsett, and Anvil Wilson, both the soldiers were gone.

"Hunted up a shady place to sleep," suggested Pat, but Anvil Wilson left the saloon and the burial detail to go hunt for them. He didn't find them. When the others finished down at the cemetery and came trooping back up to the saloon for cool ale, Anvil also returned to the *Trails End* to frowningly tell Marshal Whitsett that not only couldn't he find the soldiers, but that neither were their cavalry horses anywhere around.

That brought everyone's interest up in a dozen different ways. Jeff Stone darkly hinted that the troopers might have been involved with one or another of the outlaw gangs. Myer, noticeably pessimistic the last twenty-four hours, said perhaps the soldiers had gone out to try and contact the outlaws to inform them the gold was unguarded in Grasshopper's only saloon.

Anvil Wilson felt differently. "The young one was in no shape to do much straight thinking. I don't believe he'd have even remembered the money."

Arch said, "Just what the devil was that there squad of soljers doin' over here anyway? No one ever explained that."

"They came over to look for the outlaws," stated Anvil. "They were sent over for that purpose the same as I was. Only they went after them the army way—riding up the trail looking for a fight in the orthodox fashion, and you boys know as well as Marshal Whitsett and I know, you just plain don't ride like that in the mountains, anywhere; Apache country or any other country."

"About the others," asked Myer. "All dead, Major?"

Anvil nodded, leaning upon the bar beside the money pouches. "Marshal Whitsett and I buried them where they fell. The army'll send over a company later to dig them up and re-bury them over at the White Mountain military compound."

Old John West made a face and called upon Arch for another glass of ale. "Glad I never joined the army," he muttered under his breath, watching Arch draw his brew.

Pat Culinan returned to his current fixation. "John,

you'n these two lawmen better get your horses under cover somewhere. I'm tellin' you for a fact Fox or them other fellers'll slip into town tonight an' set you afoot if you don't."

Anvil Wilson strolled out of the saloon to stand upon the yonder sidewalk looking up and down. It was, as Pat had noted hours earlier, too quiet, too calm and hushed. As the sun began its long slide down into the saw-toothed west, shadows thickened. They made no coolness, only grey patches of dullness where the planes and angles of Grasshopper's buildings stood, warped, unpainted, rough and weathered.

Marshal Whitsett joined Anvil out there. He too looked, and wrinkled his nose. "The storekeeper's right," Carl ultimately said, speaking quietly. "They just might come to some kind of an agreement out there, wherever they are. For eighteen thousand in gold their kind would take a lot of see-sawing. It'll be dark after while, Major."

Anvil smiled a gentle, boyish smile. "No helping that," he said. "But they'll get that gold over my dead body, Marshal. As I told you on the way over here, the money is my first obligation. But now that we've got the money, my job is to catch a set of murderers." Anvil's smile was very deceptive; it belied the coldness of his practical tone. "How about you, Marshal; you want just the money, or do you want the killers too?"

Whitsett's gaze hardened. "That's a tomfool question to ask a man carrying a badge," he exclaimed.

Anvil kept right on smiling, but his eyes were frosty. "Tote up the odds," he murmured. "Two lawmen—seven or more professional outlaws."

"They're better than that," replied Whitsett, stepping back to lean his heavy shoulders against the front wall.

"Maybe those fellers inside don't impress you very much, but I know them. We can count on them to the hilt."

"Sure," said Wilson with heavy irony. "Just like we could count on those two troopers."

Whitsett lit up, exhaled and said, "Not like that at all. Like I just told you : I know these men." He paused. Wilson turned back to studying the outlying countryside again. Whitsett added something more. He said, "We've got to figure some place to hide the money. It's got to be done now, too, before dark falls. After that anything can happen."

Major Wilson turned around. "Where?" he asked.

"Myer Frankel's store. Come on."

They returned to the saloon where the conversation was heavy and apprehensive, as though each shadow added to the ones already settling over the town, made the men in Arch's place more reluctant to face the night.

Whitsett told them where he had proposed hiding the money pouches. Myer, whom they all expected to voice a quick and violent protest, merely shrugged. "I'll show you a good place," he said, arising, taking his old musket in hand and starting across towards the door. "My store is an old building. There's a stone cellar underneath it. Maybe they could find it there, but the only way they can get down into that cellar is by a trapdoor in my bolt goods department, which wouldn't be so easy with all of us around to resist. Come on; bring the pouches."

They went out right behind Myer, the lawmen each carrying one heavy canvas sack, the others walking with their heads moving, their bodies attuned for instant action. Pat Culinan was the last man inside Myer's building, and he paused just inside the doorway where he kept his vigil while the others went across to the trapdoor, which Myer lifted, and peered downward.

The cellar was small, not more than ten feet square, and was as dank and musty as a grave. Anvil Wilson remained upstairs while Carl Whitsett descended by a rotting old rickety ladder. When he was down there the others heard him muttering oaths as he blundered into ancient spiderwebs as he groped his way around. Someone offered to toss down a box of matches, but Myer stopped that.

"No fire, please," Myer said. "I got three cases of dynamite down there."

The man with the match-box clutched his incendiaries as though they'd suddenly turned into diamonds. Jeff Stone stepped over and said, "Myer; what in the name of all that's holy are you doin' storin' dynamite underneath the town?"

"Where else?" demanded Frankel. "Now and then I get a call for a few sticks. You figure maybe I should keep it under my bed?"

"Hell," growled Jeff, and turned away. The others said nothing although their faces showed that they too were disapproving.

Whitsett came back up the old ladder. Anvil extended a hand and heaved the marshal up out of the dark, musty hole. Myer carefully, very gently lowered his trapdoor and struck his palms together. As he straightened back up he looked over where old John West was leaning upon his long-barrelled Kentucky rifle watching the whole proceeding. John gazed back but remained silent. Then, as he hoisted his gun and started to turn away, John shook his head from side to side as though an unpleasant thought had occurred to him.

They walked back outside. The sun was nearly gone now. Darkness lay low in the yonder foothill valleys. It was making steady progress over the westerly, more or less open country too. There was as yet no hint of cool-ness, but most of the glare was gone. Up the northward peaks and ledges, red sunlight lay in rusty splashes along the rims and ridges.

Pat Culinan, missing all this, said in a matter-of-fact tone, "Well; I *told* you fellers, but you wouldn't listen to me." He was pointing up towards the hitchrack out front of the *Trails End* where Wilson's and Whitsett's and old John West's horses had been tied.

They were gone!

John let out a furious roar and started trotting in a crabbed gait northward up the plankwalk. "Danged cussed horsethieves," he ranted. "I'll hang every cussed one to a sour apple tree when I catch 'em. Doggone thievin' rustlers!"

Anvil Wilson didn't move. He let Jeff and Arch and Myer hasten past. He didn't even move to intercept Pat Culinan, but when Carl Whitsett came abreast, he threw out one sturdy arm.

"Go across the road and look for tracks or men," he ordered. "I'll take this side. But don't get beyond town. Maybe their notion is to put us afoot, and then again, maybe they expect us to run off half-cocked so they can slip in here and get the gold. One thing's sure, Marshal; they were right here in town when we moved the pouches. They undoubtedly saw us doing that."

The pair of lawmen split up, Whitsett turning off eastward, Anvil Wilson crossing the roadway with long strides to disappear over through a little dog-trot be-tween two sheds, heading for the alleyway which ran along back there.

Over at Arch's tie-rack John West was banging his musket butt upon the plankwalk, mad all the way through, and vividly cursing. The others, including Jeff, circled to read the sign up there, but it was impossible; there were too many fresh tracks, and the failing daylight hid what otherwise might not have been too hard to find—the tracks of the horses while they'd been led away.

Myer drew them back to the more important thing by saying, "Don't go wandering around. We got to stay close to my store. Don't forget—it's the money we got to guard, not the horses."

"That's good," stated Pat Culinan, "because we don't have any more horses to guard."

They returned to the store where Pat lamented the fact that they hadn't hidden the money up at Arch's place. "At least up there we could have a few drinks," he complained. The others paid no attention to him at all. They wanted to know what had become of the two law officers.

"Stoled like my horse," exclaimed old John West. "Whoever heard of growed men fightin' like this; sneakin' around settin' one another afoot, an' all?"

No one answered that question; beyond the windows darkness drifted in with its smothering thickness and its total hush.

Chapter Eleven

ANVIL and Carl Whitsett returned to Myer's store where the others had congregated in the pale gloom. They had found nothing, but then the others had expected them to find nothing.

"Two-thirds of a harvest moon tonight," Jeff Stone said from the darkness. "If it lights up the store it'll also light up anyone sneakin' up on us."

Myer put aside his big-bored Harper's Ferry musket and brought forth a new Winchester .25–.35 and an equally as new Colt .45 pistol.

Pat joshed Myer about that. "They'll be used weapons the first shot you fire. After that you got to sell 'em at the used-gun price."

Myer went along with it by saying, "If I'm around to afterwards sell them as used-guns, I wouldn't mind the loss. In fact I'd like it."

Carl Whitsett got a drink from an olla then joined Anvil Wilson over by the darkened doorway where both men had a good sighting up and down the empty, ghostly-lighted roadway.

"They're out there some place," Marshal Whitsett said.

Old John West, back along the southward front window said, "It's a right good place for them—out there, I mean." He straightened up. "If you boys figure to watch the front, reckon I'll go along and watch the back." As John shuffled off Arch Pennington joined him with his sixgun and his carbine.

The waiting and the uncertainty worked on them until, near nine o'clock, they heard someone coming up the southward road on a slow-walking horse. Whoever the rider was, he was whistling the cavalry song *Gary Owen*.

All of them inside the store stopped talking, stopped even moving, to listen to that lilting song being whistled down the quiet, bland night.

Pat Culinan finally said, "Soljer. One lousy soljer. This is insane. They'll get him."

Myer was more sceptical. "What would you think," he asked Pat, "if this one was to ride right smack up into town an' they never touched a hair on his head?"

Myer's implication was clear; whoever this man was, if he came through the invisible outlaw surround, the chances were excellent that he was one of the renegades.

"He'll have to be from the other side," Arch said, from back where he and old John West appeared as dark, shapeless silhouettes among packing cases. "We already know Fox an' Beeson an' Hall."

Marshal Whitsett and Anvil Wilson were out there in the recessed doorway where they'd catch first sight of that whistling horseman. They heard all the speculations of the others but offered none of their own. Finally, as the oncoming rider came to the southern environs of Grasshopper, he switched his tune and began whistling *The Battle Hymn of the Republic*, another great old marching song.

"It couldn't be a trooper," Whitsett said, against his better judgment. "You heard—they all pulled out of White Mountain."

Anvil Wilson had heard, but he had no comment to make. He was concentrating upon the emerging faint dark shape down the roadway.

The rider finally moved up where he was discernible; where melancholy moonlight and starshine mantled his shoulders and shape with a silvery dullness. He was riding a big black horse and was attired in the apparel of the range. He had his hat tilted recklessly back disclosing a youthful, dark and hard-boned face. He could have, at one time been a trooper, but according to his current attire he was not one now.

"Cover me," Wilson said to Marshal Whitsett and the others who'd slipped up towards the front of the store. Then, just before stepping out to intercept the whistling man, he said, "You fellers inside—peel off and watch the back alley. If this is some kind of a trap, they'll hit from out back while we're concentrating out front."

But evidently it was no trap, for when Anvil eased forth and came to the edge of the plankwalk, the whistling rider saw him, went silent, and reined over for a closer look. When he stopped, gazing into Wilson's moonlighted face, he said, "Well, howdy, pardner. I was beginnin' to think this place was a genuine ghost town. Where are the lights?"

Anvil, with both thumbs hooked in his belt, said, "Get down, cowboy, and tie up your horse." He said it softly, as though it were an invitation, not a command, but had there been any question about which it was, the cowboy would have found out very suddenly.

"Right glad to," the stranger drawled, and swung down, stepped ahead and looped his reins at Myer's rack. As he started around towards the plankwalk, he said, "You the only feller in town, pardner?"

Anvil stepped aside to let the cowboy precede him into Myer's dark store. "There are others," he said, waiting for the stranger to step past him. "They're inside the store; go ahead, walk on in."

But now the stranger stopped dead still and put a long, pondering gaze upon Anvil Wilson. "I'm fixin' to get me a funny little feeling, pardner," he murmured. "Is there somethin' wrong hereabouts?" He flagged with one hand—his left hand. "No lights, no noise—don't that seem sort o' odd to you, pardner?"

Anvil smiled as he gravely nodded. "Very odd," he agreed. "Now walk inside the store."

The cowboy's right hand was hanging loosely down his right side. "An' suppose I choose not to?" he asked.

Carl Whitsett cocked his sixgun in the yonder darkness. He didn't say a word or move a muscle. The stranger of course picked up that little unmistakable snippet of sound and relaxed.

"I just said *suppose* I choose not, pardner. As a matter of fact I always wanted to enter this here store." He turned, ran a slow glance across the front of Myer's building until he made out Whitsett's dull-gleaming gunhand, then sighed. "You know boys, I'm a Texan, an' us Texans has always been partial to good hospitality. Now then, mister whatever-your-moniker-is there in the doorway with that there sixgun, you just take it a mite easy, 'cause I'm fixin' to walk past you. All right?"

Carl said, "All right."

The stranger moved, keeping his right hand pointedly clear of his holstered .45. The moment he got inside, where it was even darker, he saw the wicked gleam of other guns and the pale outlines of unsmiling faces. He waited for Anvil to lift out his pistol from behind, then said, "Whooo-ee. You know, boys, I bet Jesse James never felt as downright important as I feel right now. But the difference is, I'm just a feller who punches cows for a livin' an' sort of drifts around. If you-all are fixin' t'rob me, why he'p yourselves. I got exactly seven dollars and eleven cents in my poke, but I'll trade it for anythin' you fellers got in mind, because I'm a peace-able feller at heart."

Anvil said, "Who did you see when you rode in?"

The cowboy shook his head, looking around where Anvil was standing, holding the sixgun he'd just lifted off the stranger. "No one. I seen the town from a hill southeastward, figured I'd get a little chow here, and rode on up. This afternoon though, I run across a pair of soldiers, if that's any he'p to you-all."

"One a kid," asked Whitsett, "the other an older man?"

"Yeah. The young one acted sort of vacant upstairs. He looked right through me. The older one said his friend snuck out of Grasshopper when the older one wasn't lookin', an' he had to ride hard to overtake him. They was half way over to the town of White Mountain, which I passed through this morning. The older soldier was plumb wore out."

"What else did they tell you about Grasshopper?" Whitsett inquired.

"Nothin' much, mister," replied the stranger. "Only that it was over here. They acted sort of odd, so I didn't more'n pass the time o' day with 'em. That young one give me the creeps, anyway, the way he'd look a feller straight in the eye without blinkin' or even actin' like he had his right senses. They was headin' for some army post over at White Mountain. We didn't talk more'n five, ten minutes. After I left 'em I come right along, takin' my time. Then I saw Grasshopper about sundown and headed on in." The Texan looked around. "Any-thin' else you want to know, boys?"

Anvil Wilson, all through the stranger's recital, had been carefully assessing the man. He was either nothing more than he professed himself to be, or else he was a very good actor, for an outlaw. Anvil's trouble was that he couldn't make up his mind which. He asked a question.

"Did you see any other men skulking around Grasshopper, or any loose horses anywhere around?"

"Nope," the stranger answered promptly. "Like I already said, mister, I just run on to that pair of soldiers. No one else. An' I didn't see no horses, either. Now then, boys, you mind tellin' an old trail drover just what in the hell is comin' off around your little town?"

No one answered the stranger. He looked from face to face in the darkness. It could have been an un-nerving experience for a stranger, riding into a strange town, being taken prisoner by a crew of suspicious-eyed heavily armed men in the dark who stared and fingered their weapons, and offered no immediate explanation.

"Myer," drawled Pat Culinan. "You believe his story?"

The storekeeper said, "No."

Jeff Stone walked forward through the building's rear gloom to also peer. Old John West remained back by the only rear-wall window keeping his grim vigil back there. He'd heard it all, as they all had, so now John said into the leaden silence. "We got him, whether he's a liar or whether he's tellin' the truth, so just truss him up an' dump him in a corner, an' if he's one of 'em, that means they'll have one less gun."

Jeff began nodding. "Those are about my sentiments," he stated. "Right or wrong, good or bad, we can't take chances."

Anvil Wilson still stood gazing at the stranger. Finally he handed Marshal Whitsett the man's gun, stepped over and said, "Put both your hands straight up, mister." When the stranger complied Anvil ran his hands down the cowboy's body. He found what he was looking for. Another sixgun hidden inside the stranger's shirt. As he stonily removed this weapon and tossed it over upon Myer's counter, the others turned hard looks upon the man. There was a third weapon, a pepperbox pistol secreted in the cowboy's right boot, capable of firing four small calibre bullets. It was fully loaded. Anvil also tossed that aside. In the left boot was a wicked-bladed Bowie knife.

"And that," said Myer, "makes me right. I didn't believe any of it, right from the start."

Carl Whitsett and Arch Pennington moved closer, their guns holstered but their faces like granite. Anvil Wilson, looking saturnine, said, "All right, friend; care to start all over again, and this time tell the truth?"

Before their captive could speak, however, a man's high, ringing voice called out from over across the hushed roadway in among the gloomy buildings over there. "You fellers in the store, listen to me. You don't have a chance. We got the town surrounded and cut off. We know you're in there an' we also know you got the money in there. One of you walk out with them pouches, lay them on the sidewalk over here, an' we'll ride off 'thout botherin' any of you. But if you *don't* do that you're goin' to wish to the Lord you had before dawn comes again."

For ten seconds no one spoke. John West came shuffling up from the back window. "Go on back there," Anvil snapped at him. "You too, Jeff. Keep watch back there. I think the dance is about to begin." Stone and West turned away to obey.

Pat padded on his silent feet over near the front door trying to discern where that man across the moon-lighted roadway had called from. He kept clear of both Myer's front glass window and his opened doorway.

Arch blew out a big, ragged sigh, as though, his hope

gone, he was now resigned to whatever came next. Anvil repeated his former question as though that outlaw hadn't hailed them.

"Start from the beginning, mister," he told the captive. "Or don't you feel right about tellin' the truth?"

The cowboy faced around, dropping his arms to his sides. His casual attitude was gone. He looked at them all, but concentrated upon Carl Whitsett and Anvil Wilson. "It was a good try," he told them. "In my boots you'd have done the same thing."

"Maybe," agreed Anvil. "Keep talking."

"What that feller just told you is correct. You can't get out of here alive unless they let you. The town's cut off an' plumb surrounded."

Carl Whitsett, sounding sardonic, said, "Tell me just exactly how four men can surround a whole cussed town."

"Easy," said their prisoner. "It's not just four, it's twice that many, an' they don't have to watch every building. You fellers took care of that when you fetched the gold down here and forted up in this place."

Myer sighed and wagged his head. "I knew it. I told you last night they'd get together." He waved his hands. "Maybe they were enemies before, but like I said, with this kind of money involved they'd have good reason to forget all that, at least until they got it back. So maybe afterwards they kill each other. What good'll that do us, if we're all dead when they get the money back?"

The captive's teeth shone in the dark as he smiled over at Myer. "One of you'd got a lick o' sense," he said. "This here storekeeper can see the light."

Myer snorted disdainfully at the outlaw. "You think I'm for handing the money over to you? You're a fool, my friend. You proved that when you tried coming here to spy on us, or maybe to get the drop on us. No; I wouldn't give you a lousy dime of the money. All I'm saying is that I don't like any of this; but that doesn't mean I'm for surrendering, because I'm not. You want a fight," Myer shrugged thin shoulders. "A fight you'll get." He looked around. The others nodded their heads at him.

The captive said, "You're damned fools. Two lawmen an' a bunch of storekeepers. You won't last an hour."

Chapter Twelve

THE invisible renegade across the road sang out again. "Time's up," he said. "Send someone out with them pouches or we'll blow that damned store down around your ears."

Myer suddenly moved. He went across to the shelf holding his lamp mantles and swiftly began taking the fragile little glass things down and putting them beneath a heavy counter over there. Next, he went over to heave and wrestle some heavy boards up around a drum of coal-oil. As he worked the others watched. Then Pat Culinan, moving as always without a sound, stepped in behind their prisoner, swung his .45 in a downward-chopping arc, and dropped the captive in his tracks.

The others were a little shocked, but Pat only shrugged. "Better'n tyin' him," he philosophised. "Anyway, he had that comin', thinkin' because we're a bunch of townsmen we'd let him walk in here bold as brass an' get the drop on us."

Arch and Carl Whitsett edged over near the roadway door, which hung open. Anvil Wilson glanced from their unconscious prisoner to the others. "I'll give 'em their answer," he said, "and after that you'd better be ready to fight." Anvil moved closer to the roadway door. He raised his eyebrows at Marshal Whitsett, and Carl shook his head.

"Nothing," he said. "They're across the road all right, but they're being damned prudent."

Anvil raised his head to call out. "If you want this money," he cried, "you're going to have come over here and get it, boys, and if you think six of you can out-gun seven of us inside a log building, come ahead and try it." Anvil paused briefly, then said, "And in case you're wondering—your friend's sleeping on the floor over here. He made the same mistake you're making; he thought two lawmen and a band of store-keepers had to be old grannies. He was wrong and so are you."

Anvil had scarcely ceased speaking when two guns erupted, flashing red from between the yonder buildings. Myer's front glass window shattered in a hundred pieces showering glass throughout the store. Arch Pennington was cut on the cheek and jumped forward to drop low and fire back, swearing wrathfully as he did so.

Other shots came, other lashing red flames lanced towards the store driving Carl Whitsett and Arch Pennington down low; so low in fact they'd have to expose themselves to fire back, so they were temporarily helpless.

Anvil drew and fired in one smooth motion, aiming at the nearest muzzleblast. Myer, far back and resting both elbows on his countertop, fired, levered and fired again, his new Winchester making its tight, sharp snarl each time. John West and Jeff Stone turned to yell through the noise asking whether they should come forward. Anvil yelled back telling them to stay back where they were.

The outlaws over across the road had one disadvantage in particular. Although it was customary to fire then move, so that the return-fire, aimed exclusively at muzzleblast, could not find them, this time the outlaws couldn't do that very well because there were only certain spots from which they could fire. All the town's defenders had to do was wait for a shot, then fire straight back.

Even though the outlaws had infiltrated all the buildings up and down the far side of the roadway, with the exception of the jailhouse and one or two other places which were too far southward or northward to be usable, they could still only fire out of open doorways and from broken windows.

No one was hurt inside Myer's store, barring of course that glass-cut down the side of Arch Pennington's leathery cheek, in the first prolonged and vicious exchange of gunfire. Anvil doubted too, that any of their attackers had been hit either, at first, because the firing on both sides was too angrily erratic. As he finished reloading Carl Whitsett stepped back to him and said, "For only six men they sure sound like a damned army."

Myer suddenly gave a yelp. A bullet had caught his carbine barrel on an angle, wrenching both man and gun half around, smashing the carbine's chamber and violently hurling Myer against a heavy shelf behind where he was standing. As soon as they all saw that Myer wasn't more than bruised, Pat Culinan whooped, calling over to say Myer'd never be able to get even used-gun price for the Winchester now.

Myer didn't answer. He didn't even look across where Pat was pressing back against the far wall firing out his glassless front window. He instead went straight back to the wall-rack, selected another new Winchester, and returned to the same counter to load it from the broken boxes of bullets scattered there. Myer wasn't a swearing man, nor one who exploded angrily as Arch Pennington and some of the others did; he looked shaken and grim as he levered up a load into his new gun and bent to start firing again.

Then a little lull came; the firing died down, became

sporadic, and ultimately died out altogether. It seemed that both sides were willing to have it this way for a moment.

Anvil looked back and around. Arch Pennington's shoulder was red from the blood which had dripped from his cut cheek. The others were not touched. Arch had some choice names for the unseen marksman who had caused his injury. The others were quiet except Pat, who slipped across to Myer's counter for several handfuls of cartridges. Pat said, "This could go on all night an' right now what I need is a . . ."

Arch called over, interrupting. "Hey, Myer; give him a bottle of that hoof-rot remedy you got in stock. He wouldn't know the difference as long as he can swallow it."

John West and Jeff Stone came forward to say no one was out back and they thought they should join in the fighting up front. Anvil Wilson's answer was short.

"Maybe no one's back there now, but don't think there won't be. I think we've convinced them they aren't goin' to just walk over here and get the money. They've had a bellyful out front. That only leaves the rear alley. You two stay back and greet 'em when they finally come."

John looked at Jeff. The blacksmith lifted his shoulders, dropped them, turned and walked back. John followed him, a big old scarecrow of a man carrying a musket nearly as tall as he was.

"Hey over there," someone yelled from northward and across the roadway. "We'll give you one last chance to fling them money bags out here."

Pat Culinan, back by his far-wall position, let off a splendid curse, then said, "How many of them there 'last chances' we goin' to get, boys? Come on over and get the money. It's waitin' here for you."

That started the battle all over again. The outlaws, turned fierce by Pat's taunt, blazed away. Their bullets probed inside Myer's store breaking empty lamp bases atop a high shelf, pierced bolts of cloth, smashed through tin cups and saucers, and one slug tore the back out of a drawer which held eating utensils, dumping knives, forks and spoons over the littered floor.

Myer, undoubtedly aware of the damage being done his inventory, didn't say a word. He was doggedly firing, ducking around, then firing again. He was not a fighting man at heart but he wasn't the first merchant from a western town who, when compulsion left him no alternative, knew instinctively how to fight.

A length of overhead window frame cracked loose and dropped down to bounce off Arch Pennington's shoulders. That brought more angry profanity from the saloonman. It also made him change position, because obviously someone across the road had his position under fire.

Carl Whitsett dropped down to reload. He and Anvil exchanged a look and a head-shake. There was no doubt at all that those outlaws across the road were deadly and very capable men. Also, so far at least, the townsmen around them inside Myer's store were proving themselves just as tough-minded and resolute.

"I told you," yelled Whitsett to Anvil Wilson, over the crash and thunder of gunfire.

Anvil threw Carl a quick grin, and returned to firing at flashes of orange flame across the road in among the buildings over there. He made no attempt to answer, which was just as well, because now the fight surged up to a deafening, very deadly crescendo as both sides put their whole attention into it.

Someone, over among the yonder buildings, let off a high, sudden howl, and Pat Culinan whooped again, clearly believing one of their enemies had been wounded. He had scarcely ended his triumphant yell when a slug buried itself three inches from Pat's head driving him down in a headlong dive behind a counter.

The firing began to ease off a little again. When it seemed to the defenders that another of those lulls was coming when the fighters could catch their breath and reload, John West's long-barrelled rifle cracked, making a totally different, sharper and more distinct report, back along the rear wall. Jeff Stone's carbine also erupted. Window-glass tinkled.

The others were temporarily diverted by this. Anvil, moving back, yelled for Myer and Pat, Carl Whitsett too, not to leave their front-wall positions. They didn't, but what had seemed to be an approaching lull now turned into something altogether different; half of the outlaws suddenly appeared out back, driving bullets into Myer's rear door around the lock. They smashed it, eventually, the door swung inward under violent impact, and Arch Pennington as well as Myer himself, had to jump away from their former positions because those raking slugs probed all around their areas. They ran half across towards Culinan's southward wall.

Jeff and old John worked grimly at returning shot for shot, but for old John at least, this was not possible. He did not have a rifle which could compete with a Winchester for rapid-fire, although for accuracy and sheer range, he could out-gun any Winchester which had ever been made. But this was not a battle where the fighters depended as much upon accuracy as they did upon trying to drown one another in lead.

Anvil had to dive for cover as those men out back continued to rake the inside of the store through the broken door. Out front the attack was stepped up also. Arch and Carl Whitsett fought stubbornly. Pat Culinan joined them, but once Pat had a diversion. The outlaw he'd struck down and who had been, all through the battle thus far, lying in a heap out of harm's way upon the littered floor, began to stir. Pat saw this from the corner of his eye. He left off firing, crawled over on all fours, tapped the rising outlaw on the back, and when he turned, Pat swung with his gun-hand. That time the blow caught the outlaw alongside the jaw, but it worked the same way. The man dropped into a crumpled heap and didn't stir again. Pat then crawled on over where Marshal Whitsett and Arch Pennington were savagely holding off the outlaws over across the roadway.

Then a lull actually did come, once more; even the outlaws behind the building gradually slackened their fire until little was left beyond dull echoes which chased themselves northward out of Grasshopper towards the far-away, night-shrouded hills and mountain slopes.

Arch, reloading both his sixgun and carbine, raised his head to peer around. "Anyone hurt?" he asked.

Anvil also looked, and waited for the answer to that. But no one had been hit. Myer had a purple swelling on his forehead when he'd been hurled headlong by that bullet striking his carbine, and Arch's gashed cheek still dripped, but other than those two minor injuries, no one had been wounded.

"It's a damned miracle," said Arch, grimly shaking his head. "They've thrown enough lead in here to salt a mine with."

"That worked both ways," stated Anvil. "You boys are doing yourselves right proud."

Pat had spotted a unbroken bottle of *Mother Smith's Fortified Croup Remedy* upon a shelf and was heading for it with all the single-minded solicitude of a person suffering the torments of genuine chest congestion. He uncorked it, took three big swallows, looked around, then drank the rest of the stuff. "Taste's just like Arch's whisky," he announced. "Always did have trouble with m'chest; was a real croupy baby, I was." He turned to seeking another unbroken bottle.

Old John West, calmly recharging his rifle, said, "Well sir, boys, I haven't been in anythin' so lively since the last time the Crows jumped old Big Belly's village up on the Sweetwater, unless o' course it was the time the Apaches . . ." A gun cracked. Old John's battered hat left his head, sailed the full length of the room and landed in front of Pat, over at the patent medicine counter. John spun, poked his rifle out the ruined window and let drive, then stepped clear away and began reloading again without ever finishing the rest of his comment.

Whitsett walked over to fill his belt loops and pockets from the boxes of bullets lying atop a counter. As he finished he announced that he was going to crawl up on to the roof. "They're learning something out there," he explained. "They're not going to break in here as easily as they thought. That leaves 'em the alternative of doing what they threatened: Burning us out. There's only one way to prevent that, and it probably won't work, but at least from the roof I'll be able to spot anyone sneakin' up here with a torch."

He started up the little ladder nailed to the wall. The others waited and watched. But nothing happened as Whitsett gently eased back the overhead hatch and poked his head through.

The top of Myer's building, like many store roofs in small western towns, had a false front. Otherwise though, they did not always have the kind of two-foot-high abutment which rose that much higher than the roof, which Myer's store had. It was enough protection from below to enable the deputy marshal to crawl all around, providing he didn't raise up, and also providing no one was on any other nearby roof of equal height. But since the only other roof which came anywhere near being the correct height was across the road at Pat's café, Carl could manoeuvre with a very bare minimum of risk. Much less risk, in fact, than his companions were required to face down inside the store. Furthermore, he had the best vantage place for spotting the enemy, and at least until he fired and let them know he was up there, could see everything which was going on, at least as long as the outlaws felt safe enough from overhead observation to expose themselves occasionally.

Chapter Thirteen

BUT the lull this time lasted an uncomfortably long time. Anvil, pressed to speculate by the men down inside the store, went across to the ladder, climbed up until he had his head through the roof, then softly called over to Marshal Whitsett.

"See anything, Carl?"

The lawman squirmed around shaking his head. "Too quiet," he hissed. "Too peaceful down there. I don't know where they are or what they're up to."

Anvil said, "Keep a watch," and descended back down into the store to tell the others Marshal Whitsett couldn't make out anything.

It was now past eleven, getting on towards midnight. The moon was almost directly above Grasshopper. Starlight added to the frosty brightness and seemed to also deepen the hush.

"Maybe they quit," Pat said hopefully, and Arch Pennington answered right back in a low growl. Arch was dabbing at his cut cheek. It was no longer bleeding but that didn't seem to occur to him.

"Yeah, Pat, they quit. Like a bear quits just when it rips through a bee-tree to the honeycomb. Or like you quit. Those men aren't going to quit until they have the money pouches. Make up your mind about that."

Anvil went over by the door to peer out. Jeff Stone walked up near the front of the store leaving John West back by the shattered rear window. "Myer," he said.

"I been thinking' about that dynamite you got down in the cellar. D'you know what's going to happen here if those renegades set this building afire with us—and that danged dynamite—in it?"

Myer was reloading a sixgun and a carbine. He didn't look up but he said, almost absently, "If they set fire to my building the dynamite's my least worry. What about my inventory?"

Jeff looked close. "Are you bein' funny?" he demanded. "If you are I'm fresh out of laughs."

Myer finished with the handgun and picked up the carbine. "If they fire the building we'll get out," he said. "As for the dynamite, it can't cause any more harm than a fire could. Grasshopper will burn to the ground."

From the crawl hole where Carl Whitsett poked his head through, the lawman called down. "They're over across the road westward behind Pat's café making firebrands. Someone of you crawl up here with me. We can pick them off when they try running across the road."

Jeff and Arch, even Myer and Pat started for the ladder. Anvil called to them sharply. "One of you," he said, "not all of you. Myer; Pat; come back here. Come over by the front door with me. We can sneak outside and keep watch from there for someone to try crossing the road."

Arch Pennington went scooting up the ladder with a carbine in his fist and a sixgun in his belt-holster. He disappeared through the opening out on to the roof. They could hear him bumping his way along toward the high false-front of the store.

Anvil started forward. Old John West called over to him but Anvil didn't answer. He and Pat Culinan slipped outside. It was pitch dark squarely in front of the store. Myer's warped, slab awning overhead kept any light from filtering through on to the plankwalk. Myer remained back in the doorway, down on one knee with his carbine in both hands.

"I don't see anythin'," whispered Pat, lying prone upon the scuffed old sidewalk.

"You will," stated Anvil Wilson. "Be quiet and keep watching."

It was a long wait. Pat fidgeted. Anvil and Myer were like statues, their guns at the ready, their faces turned to catch the first, slightest hint of movement out where the ghostly roadway lay, bathed in the softest of dull pewter light.

John West shuffled forward for a look around. The others heard him inside the dark store but didn't know what John was doing. Actually, having arrived at a bitter decision, old John was regretfully laying aside his long-barrelled rifle and taking a stubby carbine from Myer's gun-rack. Next, he filled a pocket with bullets, and finally, turning his back upon his own weapon, he stalked back to resume his vigil along the rear wall. He had resisted the thought fiercely and stubbornly, as most oldtime longriflemen would, as long as he could, but in the end he had bowed to what was inevitable; he couldn't throw lead like their enemies could, so he'd sacrificed his lethally accurate single-shot for one of the newfangled saddle guns.

The night ran on, dark and forbidding and hushed with a deadly, congealing stillness. Even Myer squirmed, finally, swinging to gaze over at Anvil. The larger and younger man shook his head at Myer without attempting to speak. Myer understood and looked out into the roadway again.

Finally though, they came. There were two of them at first, holding their firebrands aloft in one hand, holding their sixguns in the other hand. It was a foolhardy, bold venture, for those flaming torches lighted every yard of ground in front and behind the men carrying them. But apparently the outlaws thought their foemen were still holed up deep in Myer's store.

Either Arch or Carl fired from the rooftop just as the first outlaw sprang from behind a dark building, sprinting across the road. The bullet sliced air inches in front of the man, making him wince and falter in his stride. Whichever one of those two men atop the roof hadn't fired, did so now, taking cold advantage of the outlaw's sudden flinch. That bullet went home. Even as Pat and Myer and Anvil raised their weapons to also fire, they heard the solid, meaty sound of lead tearing into flesh and bone.

The outlaw dropped his firebrand harmlessly into roadway dust, turned to run back, took no more than four big steps, and fell. Pat fired into the corner of the building where the next man was waiting, his firebrand throwing oily, white light out upon the dead man in the roadway. A piece of rotting siding tore loose and flew out into the roadway where Pat's bullet had struck.

Myer also fired, aiming at the same corner. They also heard that bullet strike. Anvil was waiting, gun poised, for the next man to try it, but it was a vain wait. They all saw that second firebrand retreating back down the far side of the building.

Pat made a near-fatal mistake, then. He assumed they had routed the outlaws and jumped up to let off a triumphant howl. He had scarcely regained his feet when directly across the road down between two buildings, a carbine roared, coughing out a dagger of blinding light. Pat jumped a foot straight up and landed back down with a ragged curse. He spun drunkenly and fell over into the doorway nearly bowling Myer over as he stumbled back inside.

Anvil threw two fast shots down between those buildings where that invisible assassin was hiding. He either hit the man or drove him swiftly backwards out of his vantage place because no more firing came from down there.

That ended the firebrand attempt. It hadn't lasted fifteen minutes from inception to ending. It also taught the outlaws more respect for the forted-up defenders of Grasshopper.

Anvil went back to the ladder and called up to Arch and Marshal Whitsett. One of them crawled over and answered back, saying the renegades had doused their firebrands as though they were giving it up.

"Don't bet on that," Anvil called upwards. "If one of them has a strong arm he could get atop one of the buildings over there and pitch firebrands over on to one of the roofs on this side of the road."

"We'll watch," Carl Whitsett called.

Anvil went over where Myer was bending over Pat. Culinan was painfully cursing. The bullet which had come close to cutting Pat's career short, had cut across behind his left leg at the knee, neatly slicing through the flesh but not penetrating deeply enough to touch the bone. It was nevertheless a bad slash, but worst of all, it was in a very poor place, which Anvil pointed out as Myer tore up some bolt goods to make a bandage.

Pat looked up, his face contorted. "Any bullet wound's in a poor place," he exclaimed to Anvil. "How was I to know that danged whelp was right across the road?"

Anvil didn't answer, although the reply was obvious enough: This was a gunfight not a St Patrick's Day picnic. A man wasn't allowed more than one error of judgment like that, and no thoughtful man would have jumped up to celebrate a victory until after the final shot had been fired.

For a long while there was no sign of activity from the outlaws. This made the men upon the roof as well as old John West watching the rear alleyway, decidedly uneasy. Anvil Wilson took a handful of soda crackers from Myer's stock up to Arch and Carl Whitsett. The three of them discussed eventualities while Anvil stood upon the ladder with his head up through the crawl-hole. The only thing they agreed upon unanimously was that the outlaws would not withdraw.

Anvil also took some food back to John West. There by old John's window they had a little discussion. West and Anvil Wilson'd had many a long talk since Wilson's arrival in the Grasshopper vicinity. They were compatible men despite a considerable disparity in age.

"Not too many tricks left they can try," the old man said, moving up to peer out, moving back into the dark gloominess again. "Smokin' us out didn't work too good; firebrands were not much more successful. What's that leave?"

"Firearrows," said Anvil. "Maybe a couple of other tricks they haven't tried."

"Naw," scoffed old John. "These here aren't red-skins; they only fight one way an' get discouraged real easy when they try somethin' else. Naw, Major, we're goin' to get hit again before sunup, real hard, but if that don't put us down I expect they'll wait until daylight."

"Why then, John?"

"Well sir, night-fightin's never very satisfactory. It's a heap better makin' war durin' the day. With proper light a man can lie atop a knoll—or a building—and pick off his enemies slick as grease. This monkey business like tonight, all it accomplishes is to burn a few hams, raise cain with windows and such-like, but it don't kill very many men."

Anvil smiled at the old warrior. "You're right," he

conceded. "But I figure, with any kind of luck, we should all be safe enough by daylight, John. I think it'll be over and finished with by then."

West raised shaggy brows. "How?" he asked bluntly. "You got some strong medicine that's goin' to cause all their guns to jam up on 'em?"

Anvil chuckled. "No. All I've got is an idea that they've done all the attacking up to now and we've done all the defendin'. I'm aim to change that."

John West ruminated a moment while he eyed Anvil Wilson. After a time he softly said, "You mean—*us* sneak out there an' go after *them*?"

"Something like that."

West stepped around, looked out his window a moment, then stepped back up against the log wall again shaking his head. "No sense to it, Major. They're not goin' to get us in here but if we go outside, they just might get lucky. Besides, all we got to do is hold out long enough, an' they'll have to leave. Fellers like them renegades can't besiege a town forever."

"It's not that," said Anvil Wilson. "It's other things they might do—like firing the town at both ends with Myer's store in between. It'll occur to them eventually, John; they didn't have to get a man shot trying to fling a torch against the store. All they have to do is set fire to the adjoining stores. You follow me?"

West did, and he reluctantly nodded his head about it, but for some obscure reason he still hung back about slipping out into the darkness, and for a while that puzzled Anvil Wilson. He knew the old fighter wasn't afraid of men like those outlaws.

John resolved that perplexing condition himself. He said, "Y'know, Major, night-fighting can get a man killed, an' for all I know it's like the Injuns say—a man killed at night never reaches heaven. He spends all

Eternity wandering through darkness tryin' to find the way out."

Anvil saw old John was in dead earnest so he said, "You stay inside. You and Myer. I'll take Pat with me."

"Pat's hurt," the old man muttered. "No. You leave Pat in here with Myer. I'll go with you, but by grabs if I get killed s'help me I'm comin' back to haunt you for talkin' me into this."

Anvil smiled and old John ruefully grinned back. They walked up where Myer and Pat were eating dried apricots and explained what they had in mind. Myer thought it was suicidal and pointless. "We're holding them," he exclaimed. "They're finding out they're not going to get in here. What's the sense in maybe getting shot when you don't have to?"

Anvil, unable to argue against Myer's sound logic, told them his real reason. "Six soldiers are dead and one is out of his head. They're shooting up this town and destroying your store, Myer. It's only a matter of time before they roast us all out of here anyway. On top of that, the paymaster they butchered was an old friend of mine. I want them alive or dead and I aim to get them that way. You and Pat watch fore and aft. If you get hard pressed you've still got Marshal Whitsett and Arch Pennington on the roof. When John and I've slipped out the back way, climb up and warn Carl and Arch to look close before they fire. John has some idea he doesn't want to get shot in the night, and I'd feel sort of put out if I got shot by friends."

Anvil scooped up some ammunition off the counter, jerked his head at old John, then led the way towards the broken, sagging rear door. They stood back for a time, studying the yonder shadows and silvery open places where starshine lingered. There were several old tumble-down sheds out back. Their immediate goal was to reach one of them first. Anvil looked at old John and got back a brisk nod. John was ready. Anvil stepped out of the building and didn't stop moving until he reached the nearest shed. John was right behind him.

Chapter Fourteen

BACK in the doorway stood Jeff Stone. He had been across the room rummaging Myer's shelves for edibles when Anvil and John had left. Now, having heard from the others what those two were trying to do, he'd hurried back to join them, and had arrived too late.

Someone made out his murky silhouette in the doorway though. A carbine exploded up the northward alley where one of the outlaws was returning to his former place out behind Myer's building after the renegades abandoned their initial firebrand attempt. That slug was close enough to rip a long sliver out of the doorjamb and drive Jeff backwards in a big lunge.

John saw the flash of that gun and raised his carbine, but Anvil elbowed the carbine aside. "Save it," he whispered. "At least we know where he is—and so far he's got no idea we're outside. Let's keep it like that as long as we can."

The presence of that man in their alleyway, though, pinned them down for a while. They went around their shed and got belly-down to peer out and around. They couldn't make the man out right away, mainly because he wasn't moving, but also because, as the moon slanted away, darkness deepened.

There was now a slight chill to the night air. It was late. Starlight remained but it wasn't strong enough by itself to be much help. On the other hand, at least for Anvil and John West, the darker it got the better they liked it.

Finally old John said, "There!" and pointed over against the side of a building lying northward from them. "Watch now an' you'll see him move."

Anvil watched. It was a five minute vigil. The outlaw was being very cautious. He'd had half a night and better now, to learn respect for his foemen. The man was holding his sixgun in one hand, something which resembled a stick in the other hand. Anvil turned his head. "They're finally getting smart," he whispered to John. "He's got a firebrand in his left hand. He isn't going to light it until he gets close to the store. If they'd used their heads in the first place one of them would still be alive."

Then the shadowy figure up the alleyway turned and sidled along the buildings coming directly southward. As he was doing this gunfire erupted over across the roadway again. Anvil and John heard the men inside fire back. It sounded for a while as though the outlaws had decided to make another sweeping attack, but Anvil had another idea about that. The shooting was a diversion to keep every defender in the store concentrating upon the roadway while this solitary outlaw out back did what he'd slipped down there to do: Get atop one of the northward buildings and light his firebrand so he could toss it over atop Myer's store building. Anvil made his plan and twisted half around towards John.

"You sneak off to the east," he said. "Let him know you're out there as soon as you get behind some cover where he can't pot you. This diversion business works two ways. While you're holding his attention I'll try and get close enough to get him."

John nodded without taking his eyes off the vague shadow up the alley. He rose up on to one knee balancing his carbine, considered the nearest shed beyond where they lay, and finally rose up into a sprinting crouch. If it occurred to old John to ask why Anvil didn't just sneak up and shoot that outlaw, he didn't ask about it. He balanced a moment, waiting for their enemy to turn and run a long glance behind where he was, then darted out and whipped through the mottled night to safety fifty feet away. He made it without detection.

The next shack was a dilapidated old buggy shed behind the adjoining building. It was even farther off. Anvil waited nearly five minutes for John to make the run for this other protection. When he did, Anvil backed off, got up behind his shed, slipped around to the west side where the heaviest black square of night day, thrown out that far from the rear of Myer's store, and stepped out into it. He saw the outlaw flatten up along the adjoining building. There was a fire-escape ladder over there. The man's purpose became instantly clear; he meant to scale the ladder, get atop his building, then hurl his torch. Fortunately, as the outlaw groped for the first flat rung, he had both hands occupied. Anvil watched him a moment as the man tried to hold his gun, his unlit torch, and still grasp the rungs. It didn't work. The outlaw holstered his sixgun to free one hand, and that was precisely what Anvil had been waiting for.

As the outlaw turned to reach up, a stone struck the building not two feet from him. The man dropped down and whirled, flashing downwards in a wild sweep with his gun-hand.

John's stone had hit the log siding on the outlaw's left side. The man swung in that direction, his back and thick shoulders to Anvil as he swung his sixgun to bear. Of course there was nothing there, but it took the outlaw ten seconds to be satisfied about that, and meanwhile Anvil had progressed thirty feet up towards him, managing to stay in formless gloom every foot of the way. He wasn't more than ten feet off when he saw the outlaw begin to straighten out of his gunfighting stance.

Around front, in the roadway, the gun battle was still furiously raging. That was what made it possible for Anvil to make his final noisy rush; the outlaw couldn't hear him coming.

Some instinct seemed to warn the stranger at the last moment, just before Anvil's flinty shoulder struck him. The outlaw tried to whip around but didn't quite make it. When Anvil hit him the impact knocked the man's sixgun out of his hand. But this was no youthful novice, either. Caught unprepared, the outlaw nevertheless blocked the solid crash of their bodies by leaning forward instead of trying to dance clear as a less experienced man probably would have done.

For Anvil it was like striking a stone wall. The outlaw was maybe four inches shorter, but he was correspondingly broader. He had a rank smell of horse-sweat, man-sweat, gunsmoke and campfires. He recovered from the shock of surprise in an instant, swung a wild, looping blow that missed by a yard, then, instead of giving an inch, he turned on Anvil like a bear, punching and wading in.

Anvil had to give ground. This encouraged his adversary to charge in, still swinging, his little bullet-head lowered behind the curve of one protecting shoulder. The outlaw was a seasoned brawler. Anvil stepped sideways and threw the renegade off balance. He whipped over two light strikes, both connecting, but neither with much power behind them, he pawed the man off as he collected his balance and got both legs squarely beneath him. When the outlaw came in again, Anvil stepped around him on the other side forcing the man to lose ground and direction again.

That time, though, the outlaw fell back on cunning.

He didn't rush in again, instead he halted, dropped both arms and squinted through the shadows at Anvil. Then he moved, angling left and right like a cowdog bringing a recalcitrant critter to bay. His purpose was obvious; he was seeking to manoeuvre Anvil up against the building where he could nail him hard.

But Anvil was no novice at this kind of brawling either. He permitted himself to be backed almost to the wall, then dropped into a low crouch, got under two whistling swings and hit the outlaw over the belt-buckle with a solid, blasting right fist. The man's breath whooshed out; he almost dropped his guard. That blow had caught him unprepared. It had hurt him. He still didn't give an inch, though, but rather hung there blinking small, close-set eyes, and gulping air.

Anvil stepped away, swung for the man's jaw, and missed. He stepped closer and aimed again, but now the outlaw had sufficient strength again to roll with that one. It raked harmlessly up his cheek into his hair, knocking the man's hat off. He stepped clear, swung from the waist and hit Anvil in the shoulder. He was a powerful, large-boned man of about medium height, but muscled up like a bear. He had an attribute not many men possessed; he could hit just as hard with one hand as with the other. Anvil found that out when he caught a one-two series of blasting strikes that drove him off.

But that blow in the middle had sapped much of the renegade's fierce energy. He went after Anvil, but slower now, with less handy footwork, wading in swinging left and right as though by weight and heft alone he meant to batter the taller, lighter man, down. From there on it was an unequal contest. Anvil made no attempt to stand up and slug it out with the heavier, more compact man. He relied instead upon the one obvious advantage he now had; freshness. He had not been hurt.

As he moved constantly, circling the outlaw, trying to force him back to the wall, he spotted John West standing off to one side with his carbine low in both hands, pointed at the renegade. If the outlaw saw old John he gave no indication of it, but he probably hadn't seen him. He had his hands full with Anvil Wilson. Elsewhere, the fierce gun battle still raged. The sound of bullets slashing into wood was audible even out where this different kind of a fight was nearing its conclusion.

Anvil finally halted, dropped his hands and said, "Slack off, mister. You're done for."

The outlaw swore and jumped out at Anvil. He had been hurt but there was still a lot of fight in him. Anvil ducked two punches and started in for the kill. He was scarcely breathing hard at all but his adversary was gulping in air and panting. Anvil cocked a right. The outlaw raised his guard. Anvil slugged him hard with a left that travelled no more than ten inches. He jumped back in time to escape a blasting right, jumped back in and struck the outlaw under the ear as the man was twisting to get away. That time the renegade's arms dropped down and his knees wobbled. Anvil stepped away.

Old John growled at this show of humanity. "Finish him, dammit. You got him. Now finish him. Don't never feel sorry for his kind."

The outlaw turned and saw old John standing there with his carbine held crossways in front of his body. He blinked as though to focus both eyes, raised his guard again, but did it sluggishly as though each arm weighed a ton. He was beaten but he was not quite ready to concede that fact. He turned and glared, taking two steps forward. Anvil feinted him into swinging, got under the blow and fired his right. It cracked against the outlaw's breastbone with a crunching sound. The outlaw sagged, slowly dropped his arms again, and that time turned his head sluggishly to gaze around at the ground.

Old John stepped in, placed one big booted foot over the sixgun lying nearby in the churned alleyway, and smiled coldly. The outlaw cursed John and started ahead after Anvil, more bear-like than ever, shuffling his feet, rolling up his heavy shoulders, bringing up both granite fists. But it was over, all but the final strike. Anvil waited for the outlaw to reach him, then almost lazily fired his final sledgehammer strike. It cracked upon the point of the outlaw's chin dropping the man in a sodden heap at Anvil's feet.

Out front, the gunfire was beginning to slacken off. John uncocked his carbine, grounded the weapon and leaned over to gaze at the unconscious man. "Now," he muttered, "what do we do with him? If you'd just shot him it'd have been better."

Anvil stood a moment deeply breathing, then knelt, rolled the outlaw on to his back and tugged off the man's shell-belt and trouser-belt. With these he lashed his legs securely. With the man's neckerchief he tied his wrists as well. As he was getting to his feet John made a disdainful little sniffing sound.

"Still say a bullet would've been a heap simpler, Major Wilson. His kind got a way of bouncin' back from situations like this. If the cussed law courts don't set him free, he'll chew his way out of some danged log jailhouse."

"Hardly," Anvil retorted, gazing at their slumbering captive. "He'll hang, more than likely. The law's got a habit of going hard on men who kill paymasters, ambush troopers, and steal federal money."

Anvil went back to retrieve his carbine, returned to old John and watched as West flung the outlaw's .45 into the dilapidated buggy shed nearby. John then picked up the unlit firebrand and wrinkled his nose. "Coal oil," he muttered. "The thing's been soaked in coal-oil." He flung the torch away also.

There was only an occasional gunshot to break the chilly quiet now. The moon was fading fast. John raised his head like an old dog to sniff. As he lowered it he said, "Couple more hours to sunup." As Anvil stepped over the unconscious man and started on up the alleyway, John cast a final disapproving headwagging glance at their captive and shuffled off behind him.

They got all the way along to a wide place between two buildings without encountering anyone. There, Anvil looked out before moving on an angle so that, when they left the alleyway, they were still in full darkness. The occasional gunshots winking redly across the roadway were mostly south of them now, and they could hear the answering shots from Myer's emporium, but couldn't see the flashes because the next building to Myer's store cut off that view.

John waited until Anvil had eased up as near to the roadway as he dared, then said, "Major; unless you're figurin' on crossin' the roadway, we'd do a heap better to go back into the store. Out here they'll spot us after the first shot."

"We'll cross over," said Anvil, without looking around. "I just want to get an idea of about where they are, over there, before we go farther north and cross over. Don't want to run into another one; the next time we might not be so lucky. He might see *us*, before we see *him*, next time."

Chapter Fifteen

BUT they never crossed the road, either down where they were, or up at the northern end of town where Anvil Wilson had proposed crossing over.

The gunfire ceased entirely. A solitude as deep as the night ensued. Anvil waited, with John at his shoulder, for the fight to brisk up again. It never did. They stood and waited, hidden by darkness, scanning the yonder westerly buildings.

Finally Anvil said, "Now what?"

John shrugged without answering. He was sceptical of everything; of the darkness, of the outlaws, even of their chances if they should get across the road without being seen. He stooped, picked up a stone and gave it a high hurl. For a moment nothing happened, then, over across the road where the stone struck wood and rolled, only its little rattling echo came back.

"We better get back into the store," John eventually said. "This time bein' out here can't help much."

"Why not?" asked Anvil, turning.

"Because they're gone," announced old John, raising his nose. "Take a big breath."

Anvil did. He took several big breaths and didn't detect the scent of fresh dust until the last inhalation. "Be damned," he said, gazing with admiration at old John West.

John understood and said, "Nothin' much to that, Major. When I was a young buck folks more often than not didn't fight with guns. A whole cussed battle might get fought without a sound bein' made. Arrers are just as deadly as bullets. So folks got to figurin' out other ways to knowin' what was goin' on. It's dusty in summertime; four or five fellers all ride off at the same time, they stir up fresh dust. All you got to do is sniff for it." John looked around. "You ready to go back?"

Anvil was.

They returned to where their unconscious prisoner still lay, hoisted him between them and staggered back to the rear entrance of Myer's store with him. John was still dissatisfied about the way that had been handled. "He's heavier'n a cussed horse," he complained as they staggered along. "Besides, if we'd just shot him, we wouldn't have to be luggin' him now."

They got the man inside where Jeff Stone met them and relieved old John who was winded. They dragged their captive over where the other outlaw was propped against the wall and dropped him. Carl Whitsett and Arch Pennington were down from their overhead perch. As soon as Whitsett saw Wilson he said, "They pulled out. We heard 'em leaving, and just before they rode away from town we saw them."

"How many?" asked Anvil, looking around to see if all of them were there. They were.

"Four or five," said Arch, stifling a big yawn and fingering his injured cheek. "Where'd you get this one?"

"Next door," growled old John, eyeing the unconscious man. "He was fixin' to clamber on to the roof and heave a firebrand over here. I'd have shot him, but Major Wilson took him on in a dog-fight." John looked at Anvil before continuing. "I figure, after he had him, Major Wilson might have wished he hadn't. He's a reg'lar bear in a brawl—whoever he is."

Pat and Myer went over to peer at their fresh prisoner. They moved back without comment; obviously, neither of them had ever seen the stranger before.

Their other prisoner was bitter-eyed and sullen appearing. He undoubtedly had a headache; he'd been slugged over the head twice the same night by Pat Culinan, who went now to fetch a dipper of water for him. As he accepted it, the conscious outlaw said, "First round goes to the storekeepers. Wait until the next round is over."

They all stood there gazing at their captives. The conscious man drained his dipper and tossed it aside. Pat retrieved the thing and placed it upon a counter. Old John strolled over and poked the outlaw with his gun barrel. Of them all he was the least talkative but the most raw appearing. He belonged to another era, an earlier generation of frontiersmen. In John West's day prisoners very often did not survive a fight.

"What's your name?" John growled at the outlaw.

The man looked up into John's lethal old unsympathetic eyes and promptly answered. "Pete Chandler."

"And this one next to you; what's his name?"

"Rob Sutton."

John looked up. The others were just as startled. Rob Sutton was a notorious name in Arizona Territory. He was wanted from one end of the land to the other. He was a killer, a thief, and a notorious rustler. There were even federal warrants out for him on charges ranging all the way from grand theft to murder to abduction and embezzlement. He was the most notorious and wanted outlaw in the entire Southwest.

"Are you plumb certain?" John asked the man at his feet.

"Sure I'm certain, dammit all. I ride with him. I ought to know. That's why I said wait until the next round before you go celebratin'." The outlaw was hostile and antagonistic, but also, he was respectful of old John West.

Anvil Wilson walked over for a closer inspection of the man he'd whipped, but it was still too dark. He knew Rob Sutton's features from having seen them upon dozens of wanted posters. He risked a match, shielded it behind his hat and bent low.

"Well?" asked Carl Whitsett, also bending.

Anvil killed the light, put his hat back on, and nodded. "Damned if it isn't," he muttered, then turned on the other bound man. "It wasn't Sutton who killed that paymaster and got away with the money. Who was it?"

Chandler looked disdainful. "Pert Fox," he said. "A two-bit horsethief. Him an' a couple of his friends. But Rob had sent me up here to find a ranch where some old man raised steeldust horses. Instead, I ran into Pert. I used to know him over in Kansas. He invited me along on this robbery he had planned."

"So you went," said Myer. "And you afterwards rode out and told Sutton, an' he came up after the money too."

"That's about it, old man," Chandler said, throwing a casual look over at Myer. "It's close enough. Then, after Rob decided to get the money from Pert an' his pardners, we come back. But there was just this one brushpopper in camp when he snuck in, an' he pulled a damfool stunt: He went for his gun. Rob shot him in the back. After that, though, that danged Pert and his two pardners went slippin' around through the hills like a bunch of Injuns. We never even seen 'em until, when we decided to ride down here an' look around, we spotted them sneakin' in from the south. So we snuck in too." Chandler shrugged. "You fellers was here, some of you. We saw you too. Then we went after the pouches as soon as Pert got 'em back from the saloon—an' you know the rest of it."

"Not quite," Anvil said. "If you fellers had so little use for Fox, how come you to finally join up with him?"

"Fox joined us," said Chandler. "Not the other way around. He come with his hat in hand askin' Rob to let them fellers come in with us against you boys. At first Rob wasn't in favour of it, but then after we talked it over, he let 'em join." Chandler smiled wolfishly. "But I know Rob—he wouldn't have let Fox an' those other two have a dime o' that money. He just wanted them to run interference for the rest of us."

"Nice feller," murmured Jeff Stone, eyeing Rob Sutton. "Just the kind of man I'd like to have around—especially if my back was turned."

Old John West stepped away and sniffed as though Chandler and Sutton had a bad smell. He walked over to the gun counter, put down Myer's Winchester and took up his own gun again.

Anvil went across by the door and looked out. There was a steadily brightening stain beyond anyone's sight over in the rearward east, turning the pre-dawn heavens a very pale shade of watery blue-green. It was like looking up from the bottom of the ocean.

Carl Whitsett joined him over there. "What do you think?" the marshal asked.

" 'Sounds true," replied Anvil. "It fits in with what we already know. But the most important thing is that we still have the money."

"And Rob Sutton," murmured Carl. "There's ten thousand on his head in rewards. You're goin' to be a rich man when this is over."

"I'd rather be a live one," Anvil exclaimed dryly. "Besides that, though, I'm not allowed to bounty-hunt.

Give the money to Myer and Pat, Jeff and Arch. It's their town that's been whittled down stick by stick."

Whitsett nodded, then stepped out for a better look at the sky. Dawn was fast approaching. Up the northward slopes where stiff-topped pines stood in dense ranks, the darkest gloom was turning soft purple. In another half hour it would brighten steadily along towards another fresh, new day.

The others walked over, all but Pat who was guarding their prisoners because it hurt him to walk. Myer looked up, down, and around. "I wasn't so sure I'd ever see another one," he said, referring to the dawn. "Where did they go; what else can they cook up?"

"Just one way to be certain," Arch said. "Wait and see. We got to do that anyway; what choice have we got with your cellar full of money—and dynamite. You know, Myer, we got to pass a new ordinance here in Grasshopper: After this here fight's over—no more dynamite kept within Grasshopper's town limits."

Arch Pennington had torn the knees of his trousers up there on the roof, and his shirt was stiff from the dried blood which had leaked from his gashed cheek. He looked like some kind of a solitary survivor of a terrible massacre. He evidently felt like that too, because he growled something about the money being unimportant. Then, in a louder voice he said, "Those soda crackers of Myer's are fine—but gawd-awful dry. I got a fresh pony-barrel of ale opened up at my place, if any of you'd care to come along."

Carl Whitsett moved to block the exodus. "What about the money?" he said sharply, as the townsmen began moving. "We fought 'em to a standstill for that, and used up a whole night to do it. Now you fellers want to walk off so they can sneak in from out back and get it, after all?"

Jeff Stone looked the marshal right in the eye as he said, "Mister Whitsett; that's your gold, or it's Mister Wilson's gold. It damned well isn't our'n, but even if it was, I'd trade my share right this minute for one big shot of straight rye likker." He shouldered past the lawman.

The others began walking along too, all but Pat, who didn't come to the doorway to see what the others were up to until Anvil Wilson, calling after them, said, "Boys; don't light a lamp and be careful. Sutton's crew isn't running, they're just drawing off."

Pat gazed up the sidewalk briefly, made a thirsty little wet sound smacking his lips, then stepped forth and went hobbling along after his friends.

Carl Whitsett, staying back with Anvil Wilson, made an uncomplimentary comment, but Anvil said he thought the townsmen had deserved it. They weren't professional fighting men as were Wilson and Whitsett, and yet they'd done what few others had ever dared even try—they'd taken on Rob Sutton on his own terms and had beaten him to fare-thee-well.

As the two men walked back inside Pete Chandler raised his eyes hopefully, then dropped them again. At his side Rob Sutton was just beginning to heave and roll in his bonds. While Anvil stood watching Sutton, Carl picked up the dipper Pat had placed atop the counter, went over to fill it with cold water from the olla, and returned to kneel and hold it for Sutton.

The notorious killer opened his eyes, blinked fiercely, then saw the dipper and deeply drank. As he finished his last cobwebs seemed to vanish. He looked around, saw Chandler next to him, then reared back and eyed the pair of hard-eyed lawmen.

"You," he snarled at Anvil Wilson. "I remember you."

Anvil smiled with his lips only. "You ought to,

Sutton. Before you get those wraps off you'll remember me even better. This man beside me is Deputy U.S. Marshal Carl Whitsett. You'll have cause to recollect him too."

Sutton's little malevolent eyes smouldered. "You ain't hung me yet," he said. "You ain't even begun to hand me over to the law."

"Your error," said the marshal. "This here is Major Arnwell Wilson of the Adjutant General's office. He's even more the law than I am, Sutton. You've been handed over all right, don't ever kid yourself about that."

"Adjutant General," scoffed Sutton, twisting his features into an expression of deepest contempt. "Soldiers are nothin' but sittin' ducks."

Anvil told Sutton his men had left Grasshopper. He then asked where they'd been camping. Sutton swore at him. Anvil then asked who the men riding with him had been, and got cursed the second time. Wilson's face lost all hint of amiability or humour. He kept gazing into the outlaw chieftain's face.

"Untie his ankles," he told Carl Whitsett. "Then his wrists. I'm kind of sensitive about being called those names. Let him stand up, Marshal."

Whitsett refused. "He's not getting loose even for you, Major," Carl retorted. "Even if you can lick him, he's not going to get loose. I aim to take him back to White Mountain with me. We've got a real stout scaffold over there. I aim to see him hang. Normally, hangings make me kind of ill, but not this time. This time I'm goin' to stand right there below the trapdoor and enjoy every minute of it."

"You are, are you," snarled Sutton. "Well tin-badge you haven't got me to White Mountain yet. And you never will. If you doubt me, just saddle some horses an' let's try it."

Chapter Sixteen

THE outlaws did not return. Dawn came, pleasantly fragrant and cool. The marshal from White Mountain and the man from Cody County told the others to split up, half guard the store, their captives and the money, the other half do whatever had to be done throughout town. They then went together to make a careful appraisal of the town.

It had been a prolonged and savage fight. Over behind Pat's café they found at least a gross of expended cartridge casings, the marks of shod horses, and endless imprints of rangemen.

They also took that dead man out of the road, but he was the only one they found, and that made Anvil Wilson shake his head.

All of them, from Myer Frankel up to Anvil Wilson and Marshal Carl Whitsett, had the feeling they would be attacked again, probably by stealth, after daylight came. But it didn't happen. The morning wore along losing its dawn-fragrance and the coolness which accompanied that fragrance; heat began to sift in, the overhead skies turned their customary mid-summertime faded, brassy hue, but no outlaws slipped into Grasshopper to pot-shoot, nor did they come in a furious charge as Pert Fox and his men had once come.

Down at Myer's emporium where they all came together again after making their exploration, Pat Culinan, fortified now with something infinitely more masculine than croup remedy, magnanimously supplied both their prisoners, Pete Chandler and Rob Sutton, with hearty swigs from his bottle. Pat, despite his wounded leg, was in his usual high spirits, now that he'd had the opportunity to bolster them with something less stringent than gunpowder.

Anvil and Carl reported to the others: There was one corpse—the man who'd been killed trying to idiotically dash across the road carrying that lighted firebrand. Otherwise, while they did not rule out the possibility of others with wounds, they had found no more outlaws.

"But they left enough brass casings over there," said Whitsett, "to pave hell a mile."

Jeff said, "What about horses?"

Anvil shook his head, He'd seen no horses. In fact he'd seen no movement at all, horse or human movement.

Arch, who had washed and salted his gashed cheek, looked presentable again. He had shaved and changed to a fresh shirt and trousers. "Then how do you fellers get out of here with your prisoners and the paymaster's pouches?" he inquired of Anvil Wilson.

Wilson's answer was short. "We don't," he said.

"Well hell," Arch persisted. "They'll be back some time, you know that as well as I do. 'You figurin' on just sittin' here an' waitin'?"

"Nope," stated the man from Cody County. "I figure to be long gone by that time – with the captives – but I doubt if they're going to come back today, so we've got all that time to find some animals."

"I got animals," growled old John West. "They already done stoled my best critters, but I still got ten, eleven head of mares and old pelters out at the ranch."

"How do you know that?" Jeff Stone asked. "Maybe they ran them off too."

"Not likely," argued John. "No one'd run 'em off. They aren't the kind of critters even a hungry Injun'd look twice at. Still, they'll carry men. Some of us may have to ride bareback 'cause I sure don't have enough saddles, but never you fear about them critters of mine bein' unable to pack a load."

Myer shrugged. "If they can't come when you call, John, what good are they? We're *here* and they are out *there*."

West leaned on his rifle regarding the storekeeper. After a yeasty silence he thinly said, "Myer; yore trouble is you always got to think bad, never good. Let me tell you something; nothin' ever happens in this life that doesn't have two sides at the very least. Right here an' now we got *three* sides. *Their* side, your side, an' my side. On my side I say I can get out of this town, trot down to m'ranch, get them horses an' get back here without even bein' seen, let alone shot at. On your side, you're willin' to cash in already. On the side of these other fellers – they're willin' to sit back'n wait."

Myer heard old John West out before gazing over where Anvil was standing near the door, heavy arms folded across his deep chest, looking with quiet amusement over at John West. Myer said, "I wouldn't argue, John. I'm a storekeeper, not an old Indian fighter. Whatever the rest of you think we should do, I'll abide by. Only one thing I know : Sutton's scum can sit back somewhere behind a hill or among some trees, and shower fire arrows into Grasshopper, and they've been gone long enough to find the means for making both bows and fire arrows."

Pete Chandler who had, along with Rob Sutton, been closely listening to this talk, now laughed and said, "You boys're smarter'n you look. That's exactly what they're goin' to do – set this place afire, burn it to the ground, an' when you fellers run for it on foot, they'll be lyin' out there a heap safer'n they were last night, waitin' to pick you off one at a time."

Arch Pennington glowered at Chandler. "You got an awful big mouth, mister," he growled. "If you're lookin' for someone to string all your teeth into a necklace to wear around your neck, just keep spoutin' off."

Rob Sutton snarled aside and Chandler fell silent. Sutton was staring hard at old John West. John didn't seem to be aware of this, but Anvil Wilson was. He thought Sutton's baleful regard meant that the outlaw chieftain was worried over the possibility of John actually being able to get to his ranch and return with horses. To test that theory Anvil said, "John; who do you want to go with you to fetch back the horses?"

West said, "No one. When I was a young buck livin' with the Indians I learnt that one man can cover a sight more ground, trick more enemies, an' steal more horses just by travellin' alone, than a reg'lar war party can do." John picked up his rifle and patted it. "I can reach a hundred yards farther with Eloise here, than any of Sutton's yellowbellies can throw lead with those little fast-firin' Winchesters, too." He crossed to the front door and stood motionless a moment gazing out and around, then cocking a sceptical eye up at the sun. "Be back directly," he said, and walked on out.

Anvil watched how Rob Sutton's murderous glance clung to the old man for as long as John was still in sight. But Sutton said nothing. None of them did for a while after John had left them, but from their solemn expressions it wasn't at all difficult to imagine how their thoughts were running. Without even mentioning it, none of them was very hopeful. There was a lot of open country between the West ranch and Grasshopper. It was broken land, true, with dips and hills and even some trees, but because none of them would have known how to make such a trip without being detected, they thought old John was sure to be discovered—and killed.

Myer got up off a nail keg and waved an arm towards his battered shelves. "Tinned peaches," he intoned. "Soda wafers, sardines; help yourselves." He went to the olla and drank, wiped his lips and returned to his seat.

None of the others at once helped themselves to food. They lounged around the bullet-damaged store looking out into the shimmering roadway, or at one another. Pat Culinan put aside the bottle he'd brought down from Arch's saloon with him, and bent to examine his bandaged leg.

Anvil Wilson, looking drowsy because his eyelids were half down, said, "Untie Chandler and Sutton."

Immediately Carl Whitsett's brows dropped down. "What for?" he demanded.

"Because we're going to take their clothes."

Carl gazed straight at Wilson, perplexed. The others also looked mystified. Anvil went over and stopped in front of the prisoners, still with his eyes hooded in speculative thought. "Arch," he called. "Carl; give me a hand here."

Arch went over but Marshal Whitsett hung back. "What the hell good are their clothes?" he growled.

Anvil's answer was a soft drawl as he said, "Well; I've got an idea. It's probably not worth much, but I can't come up with anything better for the moment." He faced the others. "When John gets back with the horses . . ."

"Not a chance," muttered Myer, breaking in. Jeff too was strongly doubting. "Even an Indian couldn't do that, Major," he said in support of Myer.

Anvil waited, then went on. "I think he can. We're going to operate on that assumption, boys. Now then – when old John gets back with the horses, we're going to have Sutton an' Chandler ready to ride."

"In their underwear?" Pat asked, looking shocked.

"No," retorted Anvil. "As a matter of fact, Sutton and Chandler aren't goin' anywhere, but their clothes are, stuffed with straw and with sticks in the arms, legs, and back. We're goin' to sacrifice a couple of horses, tie their dummies astride, and set 'em loose heading westward. John's horses will head for home. Sutton's men are watching the town right now just like they'll be watching it this afternoon when John comes back. They'll see Sutton and Chandler make a wild break for it. I'm gambling they'll ride hell for leather to overtake them. If this idea works, that'll give the rest of us enough time to run hard in the opposite direction – towards White Mountain."

Carl Whitsett stonily regarded Anvil without a sound for almost a full sixty seconds. So did the others. It took that long for the daring of Wilson's scheme to soak in. Even Myer began looking a little hopeful, eventually, though.

Arch finally broke the silence by saying, "It might work. By golly boys, it just might work."

Before anyone else could speak Rob Sutton said, in a hard snarl. "Suppose it does? How long you idiots think it'll take my boys to discover it ain't me'n Chandler on them horses?"

"Long enough," growled Jeff Stone. "You got any better suggestion, Sutton?"

"Yeah; just one: Start prayin', because that old man'll never even get half way to his ranch, let alone get back again with horses for you."

Myer said impersonally, "Time will tell about that.

I'll admit one thing; that's the weak link in the chain."
He was looking over at Anvil.

Carl Whitsett stepped around Anvil, dropped to one
knee and began loosening Sutton's bonds. Arch Pennington took his cue from this and roughly sank down
to begin untying Pete Chandler. The others watched,
absorbed with their private speculations. When the two
prisoners were loose Arch ordered them to stand up.
They did, but none too steadily; they had been lashed
immobile for a long time.

"Take off your pants and boots and shirts," Marshal
Whitsett ordered. He accompanied that command
with a hard shove when Rob Sutton glared at him.

Chandler waited, eyeing Sutton. They were all watching the notorious renegade. Sutton cursed dourly and
began shedding his shirt. To the townsmen he said, as
he did this, "You're a pack of fools to let this simpleton
talk you into anything so crazy. Listen to me; hand
over the money bags an' set me loose, an' I'll guarantee
you we'll leave the country without comin' near your
town again."

Pat snorted. "Your word's so good," he stated, "that
I wouldn't take it on your death bed. Besides, I always
wanted to see a gen-u-wine badman prancin' around in
his underwear. I got an idea you'll look downright silly
like that, Sutton."

Pat was right. When Sutton was stripped down to his
long-johns, he stood before them looking like an un-
washed gorilla. As Myer sagely observed, it was impossible to be afraid of anyone looking so ridiculous. Sutton's face flamed red. He clenched and unclenched his
fists.

Pete Chandler looked even less fearsome; he was six
feet tall but didn't weigh over a hundred and forty
pounds. His arms were too long and his thin shanks

failed to fill out the bagginess of his underdrawers. To make it all the more ridiculous, he was still wearing his hat. Pat laughed out loud. Even Myer grinned. Jeff and Arch took the clothing over to Myer's counter. One of them said, "Myer; you got any ideas about this?"

Myer had. He got up, put aside his carbine and busied himself figuring out just how to make scarecrows out of that clothing. The others watched, passing humorous remarks, while Sutton and Chandler stood over there alternately furious and humiliated. Finally, Carl Whitsett, who never once took his eyes off the prisoners nor even smiled, ordered them both to lie down again, so he could re-tie them.

The day moved along with painful slowness. Grasshopper was as silent as a tomb. Somewhere beyond town men were lying low keeping a close watch, but none of the men inside Myer's store did more than occasionally wander up to Arch's place for a cool glass of ale or beer, or in Pat Culinan's case, a surreptitiously stolen quick shot of hard liquor. But Pat did not exceed his three-shot limit. He had his weakness, but in this time of dire peril, he also showed that he could, when he had to be, firm even with himself.

The waiting was hard though, and Sutton's jeering at the implausibility of Anvil Wilson's scheme, didn't reassure them at all. By high noon they were growing both restive and apprehensive. By one o'clock they were looking faintly doubtful. By two o'clock Arch and Myer and Jeff had taken positions by the doorway to scan the hazy, heat-lashed westerly distances for some sign of dust or movement. By two o'clock Pat had forgotten all about his drinking and had joined the others at the doorway.

It was two-thirty in the afternoon when Carl Whitsett, standing along the south wall in shadows, peering out beyond town from Myer's smashed front window, said, "Boys; look to the south – not the west. Someone's coming, an' I'd say from that dust they're coming fast."

"Lord," Arch breathed, and that was the only sound inside the store as they crowded up to watch the furiously rising banner of dust as it whipped arrow-straight for the southern end of town.

Chapter Seventeen

ANVIL WILSON moved like a man with a fresh lease on life. "Grab your guns," he snapped. "Pat; stay here and guard the prisoners. The rest of you come with me."

He led them in a headlong rush down towards the southern end of town, and it was fortunate that he did, because as soon as old John West's speeding horses were visible down the southward trace, four hard-riding armed men broke clear of the eastward hills passing down through a fringe of big trees, speeding to intercept West and turn back his horses.

Anvil ran out a hundred yards beyond town. Carl Whitsett galloped behind. So did Arch and Jeff Stone. Myer stopped part way out and changed course to get between West and the racing renegades. There, he sank to one knee and raised his carbine. He fired first because he was the first of them to be in a firing position. But the range was far too great for his carbine. Still; the shot brought the attention of the oncoming outlaws away from old John, who never once slackened speed as he ran on up.

Anvil and the others cut loose when they were able, which threw a temporary moment of caution among the outlaws, who slackened pace just long enough for John to get closer to Grasshopper's old buildings. Then the outlaws swerved to try one final desperate dash.

The townsmen and lawmen were waiting for that. They altered position to compensate for the fresh direction their foemen were taking, and blasted away again. It worked; although neither horses nor renegades went down, evidently they'd felt the breath of leaden death because they finally and reluctantly hauled up.

John began slowing as he passed the foremost outlying building. By the time he was past Myer he had his animals down to a fast gallop. Later, mid-way up the roadway, he fought the tangle of horses down to an excited and fidgeting halt.

Myer dropped back. So did Anvil and the others. They rendezvoused near the buildings at the lower end of town, and waited. The next move was up to Sutton's leaderless crew.

The outlaws walked their horses almost within carbine range then stopped and sat out there in the waves of gelatin heat, eyeing the town. They could see the defenders and John West's spiralling dun dust, but they made no additional move to interfere with either.

Carl Whitsett hooked the carbine over one arm and said, "Anvil; you'n I'd better stay down here. They'll be keyed up now that they know we have mounts. I wouldn't put it past them to try sneakin' into town like they did before."

Anvil was only half agreeable to that until Myer came over and said, "Don't worry; we'll make those dummies so lifelike they'd fool Sutton's own mother."

"I doubt if he ever had one," Arch growled. "His kind get spawned under wet rocks."

The others turned and went up where old John was stiffly dismounting. Anvil alternately watched the outlaws out there, and turned to see how the townsmen were making out. Finally, Marshal Whitsett drew Wilson's full attention to their enemies.

"Splittin' up," Whitsett calmly said, as though he'd expected this. "Going to establish a surround so they can see which way we go – when we do go." He shook his head. "Four of them left, and still the same seven of us. Doesn't make much sense, seven men running from four, does it?"

"When the seven have as much to lose as we have, it does," Anvil replied. "If that money got away from us now it'd just about guarantee at least three or four more deaths before the government recovered it again."

"And Sutton," murmured Carl Whitsett, clearly much more absorbed in the determination to get Arizona's most notorious renegade into his jailhouse over at White Mountain, than he was interested in the pay-master's gold.

The outlaws were riding off slowly, sitting twisted in their saddles watching the town. Two went around towards the east, one of them probably meaning to continue onward until he commanded a good view of the northward trace, the other man meaning to remain on the eastern side of town to make certain no one left Grasshopper in that direction. The last two men went in an opposite direction, but one of them halted before he'd ridden very far, and sat down there in the southward distance making certain no one left town the way old John West had reached it.

Anvil said, "That's all for now," and turned to walk up where the others had led two horses into that empty space northward of Myer's place and southward of the *Trails End* saloon where there was thin shade, and where they were hidden from view of the sentinel out-laws.

Myer had done an excellent job with the dummies. He'd even tied both the hats on them, and instead of the sticks which Anvil had proposed for stiffening the backs, the arms and legs, Myer had used heavy wire, which wouldn't make the dummies appear rigid. John

West stood aside with the five horses he still retained, eyeing all this with mixed doubt and admiration. When Anvil and Marshal Whitsett came up, he faced them with a sardonic little tough grin.

"Didn't figure I'd make it, did you?" he asked. Then added: "For a few seconds down there at the edge o' town I wasn't so cussed sure myself."

"Did you see anyone after you left town?" Anvil asked.

John bobbed his head. "Sure; I seen a feller lyin' atop a little grassy hill with his Winchester. I even seen his horse where he'd tied it to some sumac down in the draw behind him. In fact, if we'd only needed one critter, I could have stoled that one 'thout him seein' me do it. But I'll tell you lads somethin'; once you see the other feller, all you got to be sure of is that he don't also see you, an' that's plumb easy, if you know how it's done." Old John did not amplify that and neither Anvil nor Carl asked him about it because Arch and Jeff, Pat and Myer, now had the pair of dummies fixed atop their two horses. Myer stepped back while the others held the horses, and cast a critical glance up and down.

"What do you think?" he asked Carl Whitsett.

"It'd fool me even up close," Carl said. "How about you, Major?"

Anvil nodded, perfectly satisfied. Whatever Myer had stuffed the trousers and shirt with, gave the dummies an appearance of masculine fullness. Pat finished securing the booted feet to the stirrups and chuckled to himself as he did so. It was then slightly past three-thirty in the afternoon. The heat was a blanket of shimmering haze stretching from the northward mountain-slopes to as far southward as the human eye could see.

Arch looked at Anvil. "They're ready," he announced.

"How do you want to do it – lead 'em across and set 'em loose from behind Pat's café?"

Anvil shook his head. "That'd look too easy." He glanced across where John was still holding his other mounts, only three of which had saddles. "Carl; fetch the money pouches. Arch; you and Pat go get the prisoners. We're going to be ready to light out the second the shooting starts."

They looked at him, not comprehending. "What shooting?" one of them asked.

"The shooting we'll do just before we release the mounted dummies. It's got to look as though Sutton and Chandler fought their way clear. We'll fire in the air over behind the café, which will bring them over to that side of town – I hope. Then set the dummies loose, run back here where John'll be holding our horses, and strike out for White Mountain as hard as we can ride."

Carl, Arch and Pat started off, bound for Myer's store. Old John and Myer stood there faintly grinning. Anvil Wilson, who usually responded instantly to humour in others, did not now do so. He walked out into the roadway and looked southward. That outlaw was still down there keeping his grim vigil. Anvil angled farther over so that he could see northward. The man up there was farther out, in some thin chaparral shade, but he too was discernible. Anvil went back where Carl and his companions were returning. They had Sutton and Pete Chandler in front of them gimping along over the hot ground on bare feet. Carl had the pouches over his shoulder and his sixgun swinging easy in his right hand. He was taking no chances whatever.

Sutton and Chandler halted when they saw the dummies. Neither said anything but their expressions proved that they were chagrined at the resemblances.

"Think it'll work?" Arch asked Sutton.

The outlaw chieftain cursed. "Not in a million years," he snarled. "I don't keep idiots in my crew." But as Sutton went past under the prodding of Whitsett's six-gun, he craned for a closer and patently interested look at the mounted dummy wearing his clothing.

Anvil jerked his head at old John, who promptly led forth two of the bareback horses. "Get up," John growled at the outlaws. "Personally, I think it's a down-right shame, my horses havin' to pack double in this kind of weather, when two bullets would do the job so much better'n botherin' with you two."

Sutton and Chandler mounted, winced when they settled over two boney backs, and turned to watch as Anvil, Pat and Arch started across the roadway leading their mounted dummies. Myer started to follow them but Carl Whitsett called him back. Carl had those canvas pouches at his feet. He also had their two rene-gades to watch. He did not mean to take one single chance.

Pat hopped along on his injured leg as though scarcely conscious of his wound. Arch too, was near to grinning. Anvil alone looked pensive and grave. They looped both sets of reins with just enough slack to allow both horses to set their heads to run, then made some last-minute adjustments. Anvil tested the dummies to make certain their ropes and wires would keep them upright. When he was finished he drew his sixgun and stepped back. At once Arch and Pat did the same. The horses looked around, bewildered because there was no actual restrain-ing hand upon their reins.

Anvil said, "Arch; give them a cut across the rump." Arch did. Both horses jumped and snorted. Anvil fired into the air. Both Pat and Arch also fired. If the horses had needed any additional encouragement after being struck, those gunshots offered it. They broke away in a headlong rush out through the sheds and shacks behind Pat's café, heading for home as tight as they could run.

Arch whooped and fired. So did Pat. Anvil did too, but he also ran a searching look out there where one of those outlaws had ridden to keep a vigil to the west. He didn't see the man until, southward somewhere, a man's high, keening shout rang out. Then he saw the westerly renegade. Only he wasn't alone, now, for evidently he'd been more southward of town than westward, and had called to the southward watcher before starting in hot pursuit. That pair of horsemen broke around the lower end of town riding twisted to fire back towards Anvil, Pat and Arch, their intention evidently being to divert what they assumed was a fierce attack upon Chandler and Sutton.

Anvil stood to briefly watch; to make certain the plan was working, then he stopped firing, turned and called to the others, and reloaded his sixgun as he trotted back across the road where John and Myer and Carl Whitsett were tensely waiting.

"Worked like a charm," bawled out Pat Culinan, reaching for the reins old John pushed towards him. Anvil gave Carl a hand lifting the money pouches and securing them to one of the saddles. That was all the time they wasted. By the time Carl got astride the saddled horse with the money bags, the others were also mounted. John led out, weaving back and forth past piles of discarded debris out in the eastward alleyway to the very edge of town. There, slowing his horse to a walk, he made cautious headway, looking around for that outlaw who'd been stationed out there. The man was gone.

"Damn," muttered old John in wonderment. "I guess it did work like a charm at that." He looked around at the others, let his shrewd old eyes linger a moment in silent triumph upon Rob Sutton, then eased his horse over into a steady lope heading due east towards a thin stand of pines. "Keep an eye on our two guests," he cautioned the others. "Be a shame to have them try'n to run off so's I'd have to pick 'em off with m'rifle."

They left Grasshopper behind. Nothing happened; they didn't encounter a single rider; no one fired at them; the heatwaves sluggishly parted as they ran along, and eventually, as they were passing through that shielding tree-fringe, Pat laughed aloud out of sheer exuberance – and relief.

It was hard on their animals. Aside from the fact that, as old John had told them, these were old broodmares and retired geldings long in years and short on wind, the heat was murderous, the horses were overloaded, and the terrain was rough.

They could have dropped southward but old John, who was leading, never made the effort, preferring to stay more to the northward where there were arroyos and stands of protective trees. He did, however, halt after they'd been riding for nearly a half hour.

"We'll make it soon enough without killin' the horses," he told them, and turned to drift back where he halted among some bull-pines to study their backtrail. He only sat back there for a moment, then returned to the others shaking his head. "They're comin'," he announced. "I reckon they had better horses than we figured. 'Must have overtaken the dummies about a mile or two beyond town." He twisted to point. There was a hot streamer of dust jerking to life back a few miles, heading straight in the direction their horsetracks were leading.

"Reckon we won't have as easy a passage as I was

beginnin' to figure on," the old man grumbled, and eased out again. "We'd best get to movin'."

They did not hurry though, until John led them down a shady arroyo which angled more southward than eastward. It was cool enough for them to lope another mile before their arroyo rose up and dumped them out upon the shadeless plain again.

Chapter Eighteen

THEIR horses began tiring after four miles. Anvil and Carl Whitsett were equally as concerned as were the others. Jeff Stone, who had Myer riding behind him, got down and told Myer to get into the saddle while he trotted along beside. They continued on in this fashion for a short distance more, but the heat was as punishing on Jeff as upon the horses. His trot slowed to a shambling walk while water ran off him in rivulets.

It did not appear they would make it, after all. Their scheme had worked well enough, but their failure was due, not to the men at all, but to their animals. John apologised, chagrined and troubled. They told him he'd already done more than any of them had done.

Sutton's men gained steadily, but they too had need for a respite long before White Mountain came into view, which permitted the fleeing riders to at least hold their lead a while longer.

"This is the longest ten lousy miles I ever rode in my life," Anvil Wilson told the others where they paused briefly in some hot shade among a ragged stand of fragrant trees.

Rob Sutton, grotesquely sitting atop an old sway-backed steeldust mare and sweltering in his underwear, said, "You'll think it's worse'n that when my boys catch up to us, mister."

Old John's answer to that, plus his baleful glare at Sutton, turned the outlaw silent. "If they *do* catch up, you'll be the first one to wish they hadn't, Sutton. I damn well promise you that."

Pete Chandler's courage was seeping away. He said, "Listen, fellers; it was Sutton who killed that paymaster and made up the ambush that dropped them soldiers. All I did was ride along and . . ."

"Oh shut up," Arch growled at Chandler, wiping off sweat. "It's bad enough bein' out in this heat without havin' to listen to you. Just shut up."

They went on again as far as the next stand of trees. John was choosing their route with two things in mind: The need for shade and relief every few hundred yards, and the increasing strong possibility that they might also need shelter to fight from.

Dusk did not arrive until eight o'clock in the evening. Sundown was only an hour or two earlier. Full darkness did not blanket the range until nine o'clock. It was by this time close to five in the afternoon. The sun was dropping low but the only difference this made was that instead of being punished by overhead heat, they were getting it against their backs and sides, and also, when they stopped and looked back, in their faces.

Old John suddenly straightened in his saddle. "I got an idea," he said, and turned eastward again heading for some of the wildest, most desolate country in the White Mountains. In fact, if he rode long enough in that direction he'd lead them past the town of White Mountain, down the yonder watershed into Old Mexico.

But he didn't do that. In fact he didn't lead them more than one more mile before he swung down, scrambled up a low hill covered with brush, and raised up when he reached its crest to look around. Then he returned, and still without explaining, took them down through one of the most thorny, brushy, skimpy little trails any of them had ever ridden before, through hills that closed in on both sides and also closed in from behind, making Pat and Myer exchange an uneasy glance.

This trail, obviously, had seen recent travel, but the very way it had been hacked out, as well as its hidden, gloomy twists and turns, put them all in mind of those oldtime paths the Indians made, which enabled them to swiftly pass back and forth through the mountains on trails very few white men ever saw, let alone came across.

Anvil Wilson finally pushed on up where the trail was wide enough, and got beside old John. "Where does this trail go?" he asked.

Old John just grinned and raffishly rolled his eyes. "You'll see danged soon," he said, then pushed ahead where the trail narrowed down again.

Anvil dropped back. Carl Whitsett asked him what West had said, and when Anvil repeated John's words, Carl began to darkly scowl up at old John's back on ahead. They were by this time riding at a walk; the terrain would not permit any faster gait.

Finally, John stopped, raised his left arm to halt the others behind him, twisted half around and smiled at them looking less than ever like someone about to be ridden down and exterminated by four oncoming renegades on good horses.

"We made it," John said, pointing back up where the dust from their pursuers was visible slightly more than a mile off.

"Made what?" demanded Arch, scratched and sweaty and on edge. "Made where?"

John winked, lifted his rein-hand and dropped down the trail another dozen yards and came out into a large grassy clearing where about a dozen brush-shelters stood. There were Indians down there. Some were emerging from the brush-shelters, others were already standing out in their campsite-compound, armed and curious, gazing over where the battered riders on their scarecrow horses were coming out of the brushy hills.

"From the damned fryin' pan into the fire," muttered Pat Culinan. " 'Paches, an' they've seen us."

Anvil and Carl Whitsett rode together across the clearing. The others also closed up, riding carefully and upright. There were no more than ten bucks down there, but that was enough. They were a beady-eyed, short, muscular band of men with straight, rank black hair and powerful arms and shoulders. One of them was old. It was towards this bandy-legged *anasazi* John West set his course. The moment he halted with upraised gun-hand, palm forward, he began biting off short, guttural sentences, and smiling like a madman. Gradually the old Indian also smiled, but his expression was the smile of a wolf closing for the kill. He kept right on smiling as he turned, barking orders to the younger men. In a twinkling the younger men were gone into the brush.

John got stiffly down. He and the ancient spokesman for this ragged little band, laughed at each other and pumped arms. They were obviously old friends. They were also just as obviously a raffish pair of old schemers, for when John led the old buck up where Anvil and Carl Whitsett stood, with the men from Grasshopper, around their prisoners and the horse containing the money pouches, the old Indian's fathomless, bright, fierce eyes saw the money bags first, then the captives, and he said, broadly smiling. "My men catch others, bring them here. You make present of other men's guns and pants."

Arch Pennington muttered. "Gladly, Chief. You can even have their horses for all I care."

"Hey," spoke up old John, suddenly no longer smiling.

"Those are my horses them fellers are riding. They stoled them from me. Where do you get off givin' away my . . .?"

"I'm sorry," Arch hastened to interject. "I didn't know they were yours, John. I'm plumb sorry."

John wasn't placated and the old Indian's grin slipped a little until Anvil Wilson came into the breach with a solution which salvaged the situation. "They've got other horses," he told them all. "The animals Sutton and Fox first rode into the Grasshopper country. We can get them and hand them over."

"*Enju,*" exclaimed the grinning old Apache, who understood more English than he could speak, which was typical; border-country Apaches usually spoke Spanish as their second language and had difficulty speaking English even if they'd been to a mission school where English was constantly spoken. "Now you come," the old spokesman said, pleased that the arrangements had been made, and led them all over to a particularly large brush-shelter where they saw Mexican saddles, bridles, sombreros, and other spoils hanging, which they affected not to see, for it was now apparent that this was one of those marauding bands who raided over the border when the spirit moved them, bringing back whatever plunder struck their fancy.

Anvil looked back once, and found Carl Whitsett, Arch Pennington and Jeff Stone doing the same thing. Back there through the intensely gloomy and brushy hills, Sutton's remaining outlaws were riding straight into a trap.

John said, "Marshal; you got to do me a favour."

Carl looked critically at the old rancher. He knew what that favour was, and in his job Indians like these were anathema; they kept the border-country on edge. They also kept the Mexican Government constantly angry at the U.S. Government because Apaches were the charges of the U.S.

"You got to forget you saw these folks here, Marshal," old John said.

Anvil Wilson, also eyeing old John, asked a question. "Did you know they'd be here, John, or did you just hope they'd be in this rancheria?"

"Well, no, Major, I got to be truthful. I knew it."

"And," said Carl Whitsett. "You knew they'd been raiding over the line, John. You even knew they'd have plunder."

John squirmed. "Well now," he said, looking uncomfortable. "You got to understand, Marshal. Raidin' Mexico's their livelihood just like raisin' horses is mine and keepin' the peace is yours an' . . ."

John broke off when, without a sound, six or eight impassive Apache bucks strode out into their secret meadow leading four horses with rumpled riders tied upon them. They had accomplished their ambush without a shot being fired or a yell being raised, which was the Apache way. There were no better ambushers on earth than Apaches. Sutton's men looked more bewildered than bruised. They had been disarmed and one man who'd been wearing a fairly new pair of boots, was also barefoot.

John West said, "Marshal; there are the rest of your outlaws, trussed up an' delivered all in one piece. You also got your gold, plus Rob Sutton. Now leave me to ask you one question: Could you have accomplished it without my friends here?"

Carl was honest. "No, John. I probably might not have even gotten back to White Mountain alive, let alone with the money and Sutton."

"Then," stated John, pressing to make his point. "You goin' to snitch on my friends for bein' here? Sure they just come up out'n Mexico. But you can see, they didn't bring back no slaves. They're right decent folk that way, Marshal."

Carl's stern features relaxed as he watched the impassive bucks lead up the frightened prisoners and hand their reins to Myer and Arch, Pat and Jeff. "What friends?" he asked.

John screwed up his face. "Why, these here Injuns; what friends you think I been talkin' about?"

Carl gazed around and raised his eyebrows at Anvil Wilson. " 'You see any Indians, Major?" he softly asked.

Anvil gravely shook his head. "Not a one, Marshal. All I see is a herd of prisoners with prices on their heads, those money pouches I've been hunting for, and the lads from Grasshopper who helped us get both. That's all I see, Marshal."

John's creased old features curled into a broad smile. "I'll say good-bye for you boys and we can head on down to White Mountain."

The Indians were delighted to earn good guns for such a small favour. There had of course been risk, but to a people accustomed to deadly peril almost from birth, one simple ambush was hardly considered a risk.

Anvil though, had to reassure their old spokesman he would personally make certain the horses were delivered over at John West's ranch where the Apaches would move their camp and wait. After that, the old man grinned until it appeared his eyes would entirely disappear in wrinkles, and vigorously pumped the arms of both Anvil Wilson and Carl Whitsett, stepped back and threw them a fine Mexican salute as they rode off southward, down across the hidden Apache rancheria.

Old John led out again. He knew the White Mountains as well as he knew the inside of his own hand. They cut a high trail and breasted a scaly ridge where winter winds scourged the soil almost down to bedrock, and from that eminence could see the town of White Mountain far below and southward.

Anvil gazed at their fresh captives. The Apaches had lashed their arms behind them. Every time old John led them through one of the interminable brush patches the barefoot one cursed with full-flowing pain and abandon. Chaparral thorns were often two inches long and dagger-sharp.

Not until they were down out of the hills with the sun nearly gone did Rob Sutton speak. He had shared with the others a few bad moments back there at that rancheria, now he said, "Listen, boys; what'd you say to each of you earnin' a thousand dollars just by untyin' my hands and lookin' the other way for five minutes?"

John West answered right back before either of the lawmen had a chance. "I'd do it for one dollar. In fact I'd give *you* a dollar."

Sutton glared, not comprehending. "What's the matter with you, old man," he growled. "The sun scramble your brains?"

"It must've scrambled yours," retorted John, "if you think for one minute there aren't 'Paches slinkin' along behind us right this minute, waitin' for one of you renegades to get away."

Sutton turned to throw a swift look over his shoulder. As he straightened forward again he growled, "Forget it. You wouldn't know what to do with that kind of money anyway."

They came across the last landswell, left the brush-country behind, and saw their first cattle not far from the visible outskirts of White Mountain, where a flag flew from the mast of an old army post on the northern-most outskirts of town.

Pat Culinan was suddenly struck with the impropriety

of leading Sutton and Chandler through town in their underdrawers. "Hey, you fellers," he called out. "We got to put some pants on them two. It's not seemly, what with womenfolk an' kids around, to fetch men into town without their britches."

Anvil had the answer to that as they entered the outskirts of White Mountain, finally, having survived everything the outlaws had hurled at them, plus a number of other obstacles such as heat and sleeplessness and borderline Apaches.

"Womenfolk might be a little shocked, and the kids might be too," Anvil said. "But there's no better way I know of to reduce a notorious bunch of badmen to jelly then to get them laughed at. And John; if you don't think killer Rob Sutton isn't something ludicrous, just take another look."

They were all grinning a little, filthy and exhausted as they were, when they started right down through the main part of White Mountain with their captives — and their canvas pouches.